The Goolwind Tales

Ricky Hayes

The Goolwind Tales by Ricky Hayes
Book One
Published By Ricky Hayes – DBA Publisher's Brew

ISBN-13: 979-8-2-18-98640-7
PAPERBACK
EDITION NO. I

CREDITS:
Editors: Ricky Hayes, Melinda Russell
Cover Design: Ricky Hayes

PERMISSION REQUESTS:
Website: publishersbrew.com
Author Page & Portfolio: publishersbrew.com/rhayes

SOCIAL:
Facebook: facebook.com/publishersbrew
Instagram: instagram.com/publishersbrew/
Tik Tok: @rickyhayes_author
Linktree: linktr.ee/rickyhayes_author

Contents

Essend
Walrook
Flemder
Autumnwich
Outlands
N
W
E
S

Essend
Ogrin Forest
Byre
Arval
Dundon
Goblin Tribe
Gnoll Tribe
Gnoll Tribe
Colbor
Gomhader Forest
Goblin Tribe
Gnoll Tribe
Shroo
Lem
Tolu
Holprice
Goblin Tribe
Pratop
Bonol

W
N
S
E

Casters and Kingdoms

Two children stood in the upper room of the monastery, a library filled with various books of knowledge and spells, many of which they had yet to read in the comforts of their father's study. Now, they stared at the Head Caster, hardly hearing his words after he began to explain that their father was lost. More than a year had passed since their father left the Holprice monastery, and nine months since the Head Caster last received word from him. The Head Caster did not speak of their father's mission but held his face sorrowfully toward them both. Placing his hands on each of them, he did his best to keep them at ease. Yet Avaleigh, a young girl of twelve, could not keep her tears from shedding. Her younger brother, Hayden, a boy no more than nine, followed her lead in sensing the fear that now overwhelmed them.

Left with their thoughts, the Head Caster slowly made his way out of the room and shut the door behind him. The two young children held loosely to their staffs, as each of them had received them as a gift, both children celebrating their birthdays the month prior—Hayden toward the mid of the month while Avaleigh's fell just upon the last day. Both had found it difficult to celebrate as worry burdened them often, and now their distraught choked them ever tighter. While each showed excellent promise in becoming powerful casters, they suddenly fell into one another's embrace wondering what would become of them.

Now, what is a caster you might ask? They certainly are not any sort of ordinary folk, but masters of sacred magical arts and usually hold a magnificent sense of will. And the two children holding one another were anything but ordinary, even among casters. Their bloodline held ancient ties, much like their uncle, the Head Caster of Holprice's monastery. Yet the bloodline spoken of came from their mother's side—the only line known to be able to sense Tremors of Power, magical energies invisible to everyone else, and are said to quickly enhance a caster's abilities. Being able to find them is a task more difficult than strengthening one's abilities through practice and study. However, Avaleigh and Hayden were drawn to them, already seeking out several that surrounded the monastery during their first years of study. They were what many would refer to as precocious or wunderkinds.

While still inexperienced in their abilities, Avaleigh and Hayden were growing their power exponentially faster than other casters their age. It even caused them problems with the other children, as they were bullied for their ease of mastery. It cost Hayden a tooth at one time as he was sucker punched during an argument by his once best friend who angrily admitted his jealousy of Hayden. Luckily, the tooth was already loose, making room for a more permanent one peeking through. The event took place at his seventh birthday celebration no less. Afterward, Hayden made sure Avaleigh was his only friend. For she too felt outcast by her peers, with vicious rumors and unkind pranks.

Their uncle had recently pulled them from learning with the others—not for their safety, but for the protection of the other children. The Head Caster was quite aware of the growing abilities of his niece and nephew, taking notice that they were even outpacing him when he was a child. He did not wish to risk them losing their temper and performing something rash. He had loved helping his sister-in-law and his brother care for them over the years and enjoyed being their teacher. He took a personal interest in instructing them what he could about the world, knowing they would likely travel to the other kingdoms.

At so young an age, it was no secret in Holprice that the two youngsters were likely already prepped well enough for whatever Goolwind would throw at them. Although, perhaps Avaleigh's confidence needed a little work, and Hayden's smugness needed to be knocked down a peg. Yet the power they could cast showed great promise, even frightening some in the kingdom. It steadfastly became apparent that Holprice would not hold them forever. For now, the children's home was in the city, just one of the major metropolises in the kingdom of Essend. Farmland and several hamlets encircled the keep of the city that held the monastery dedicated to producing and teaching casters.

Essend is known for one particular magic—Tempest, which focuses on harnessing chaos into order. Such spells naturally grow more powerful over time with practice and study, but mostly with age. It is common for a caster to choose one primary and one secondary spell to hone their skills. Tempest spells also carry practical application properties to understanding the growth in the knowledge of how a caster's power in this discipline is fundamentally heightened.

Avaleigh learned to be a natural with "Crashing Tide" and chose it as her main focus in the Tempest discipline of magic. The spell creates and duplicates water from moisture, whether from liquid or in the air. Growth in this spell allows the caster to essentially make water do whatever they want, including walking on dry land. Her secondary spell of choice was "Stormy Gale," the ability to create incredible gusts of wind. While not entirely useful for beginners as it is sort of like blowing air in someone's face—combined with her primary focus, a caster could grow the spell's capabilities to generate clouds and pour down flooding rainfall as well as enormous chilling winds to either frost or fling things high into the air.

Hayden's natural ability fell toward "Thunder Strike," the ability to powerfully build up electrical currents and launch them at anything. With practice, the spell becomes deathly charged on impact. "Sinister Cyclone," Hayden's second discipline, allows a caster to create a destructive twisting wind. And as a caster's power grows, so does their ability to generate larger-scale cyclones. Coupling this with Thunder Strike allows the caster to also electrocute whatever is caught up in the cyclone winds.

Their uncle had already left the room after giving them the news of their father, knowing the time was drawing near for their real world trials. He had overheard them many times talk about exploring the beyond the walls of Holprice. And it would seem the love for their parents would drive them to venture out. Yet he remained unsure if they were ready to pick up the quest where their father and mother left off. He stared at a map of the world tightly stretched out on a tapestry just outside the library door—the minacious world known as Goolwind.

Made up of four separate kingdoms, Goolwind has four major islands, each one divided by the treacherous tides of the seas. The islands make up a large diamond pattern in cohesion with one another. Anything beyond the four islands is considered the Outlands—vast mainlands filled with much larger dangers and unknown predators. Those who have ventured there have either been lost to the wilds or likely met their doom.

The four kingdoms; however, share a harmonious peace to help one another prosper despite the kingdom islands holding many dangers of their own. It is not uncommon for casters of each kingdom to venture to the other islands to learn the different types of magic from one another—Tempest, being of Essend, Dusk, being of Walcook, Conjuring, being of Autumnwich, and Nature, being of Flemder. Two other disciplines are held throughout the kingdoms and vary in abilities among casters—Gravity and Allay (Healing). These two disciplines hold a high degree of difficulty and are seldom taught to young casters.

Over the ages, knowledge of many spells and disciplines has been lost but a few casters have pursued such secrets utilizing archeology and historical research. While no major discoveries have been uncovered over the centuries, whispers of a secret book containing knowledge of the ages have reached the ears of many folks for many generations. The dangers surrounding such knowledge are both unknown and can bring about lethal encounters for those searching for the book.

However, the potential to uncover any measure of secrets could be found throughout the four islands. Many casters who take an interest in adventure spend their days not only practicing casting but also studying geography to better understand the landscape of where they desire to explore. Every caster is required to know the fundamental layouts of each of the islands, including their own, as well as certain customs of the other kingdoms.

Essend consists of three major cities—Colber, Dundlen, and Holprice, Colber being the capital. The kingdom's emblem is that of a stag, flying the colors of gold, sapphire, and highlight black. The island is mostly rolling foothills, evergreen trees, plenty of rivers, and small lakes. Its highest peak is about a five-day trek for even the most experienced of adventurers. Among the hamlets spread throughout the island are monasteries dedicated

KINGDOM OF ESSEND

to upbringing young children in ways of spell Tempest casting, with Holprice holding Essend's head monastery. Essend's most dedicated and prized students become connoisseurs of Tempest—the philosophy being that mastering the fundamentals of harnessing the power of the weather allows one to be the most formidable of casters.

Flemder is made up of small villages, hamlets, and farmland with one major fortified city known as Breg. The kingdom's emblem is that of a boar intertwined with tree branches, flying the colors of crimson and grey It is built of stone and iron, and located at the heart of the island with mountains and valleys portraying some of the most majestic waterfalls ever seen in all of Goolwind. Rivers allow for the finest farmland and gives Flemder

KINGDOM OF FLEMDER

one of its largest commodities in trade. Residents of the hamlets are dedicated to farming and trade skills; they also train their children in Nature Spells. Should students show great promise, they move on to continue learning advanced Nature Spells and even take part in pilgrimages to other kingdoms. .

Autumnwich is a war-torn land inhabited mostly by craftsmen and miners living in the vast mountain ranges. The kingdom's emblem is that of two iron hammers crossed over one another atop a shield, flying the colors of ash, silver, and burgundy. Most homes are carved into the mountainsides and dwellings continue to increase as families grow and burrow further. Many families have

KINGDOM OF AUTMUMNWICH

skilled hunters and timber harvesters who go out into the wilds to gather wood for trade and meat for families. The reason for cave-dwelling is due to the large population of Gnoll tribes, which often war against one another as well as the folk of Autumnwich.

Gnolls are a vicious war-minded but also simple-minded race of beasts that are hyena-like yet humanoid. They are known throughout the four kingdoms. Though highly aggressive, Gnolls are notorious for being prone to fighting amongst themselves and love to enslave others. The majority of tribes are mainly found in Autumnwich and do not have a love for caves or those who dwell within them.

GNOLL

Walcook is a kingdom united through dominant trade, richly dominating the other kingdoms in selling its goods, and has three major cities, Shaul, Carwal, and Wame, that harbor exceptional merchant guilds.   The kingdom's emblem is that of a large tree covering a moon, flying the colors violet and white. Walcook is mostly a green, rocky region of rolling foothills and meadows, with one large river

KINGDOM OF WALCOOK

running south to north, and one large forest surrounding the river. Casters specialize in Dusk spells, and as such, the region is made up of a variety of thespian and performance guilds as well, including ones that travel to the other kingdoms to seek fortune and renown. The kingdom is known for its historical traditions of festivals that incorporate celebrating, "The Days of Dusk," "Days of Champions," and twenty-four days of "YuleTide,"—a holiday celebration twice as long amongst the other kingdoms. Walcook is also famous for its craftsmanship of lanterns, which become part of their "Festival of Lights" depicting the end of winter and the beginning of spring.

As such, Avaleigh and Hayden had waited one arduous month for the first day of spring to bloom in Holprice. No one knew what they were planning to do. No one would have dared to venture a guess— well, perhaps one—they would leave Holprice to go in search of their father. They had determined to learn as much as they could of their father's mission during the last month of winter. With his big teary eyes, Hayden did not have much trouble convincing their uncle to at least divulge some small details. The boy prided his magnificent performance in shedding tears and then drying them in an instant, even boasting somewhat irritatingly to his sister. However, she fed into his ego with a few pats on his back.

There was a spellbook that their uncle would not name, but it was likely the one few sought to find. He did mention it was an ancient book of sorts, something the monastery of casters in Essend wanted to keep secret and guard against falling into the wrong hands. It made Hayden anxious to leave, as he loved tales about the secret book of lost casting knowledge. And now, he became antsy of the thrill, even curious as to facing danger.

A couple of days before their planned departure, the two children took advantage of the people's generosity, claiming to be collecting small donations of food for those who were having financial difficulties. It nipped away at both of their moral upbringings, but they had convinced themselves of the dutiful cause. Their father was alive. They just knew it. Though the same they could not surmise about their mother, Jennifer of Holprice, though each hoped the same to be true. She had disappeared four years prior, likely in search of the book as well.

With wooden staffs in hand and all the gold they could muster in their pouches, they set off without a word to their uncle. They had left a letter for him at the post station, marked to be delivered within the next week. The Postmaster thought nothing of it, seeing that the children had fibbed about it being a card to surprise the Head Caster for his birthday.

When the two approached the city gate of Holprice, the guards were not as attentive as they should have been. They slipped past them, and out into the wide-open kingdom of Essend, deciding to scurry their feet in the direction of Colber, the capital. Perhaps they would see the king and queen, which excited Avaleigh more so than Hayden, who focused his attention on Colber's fine dining. Despite his thin appearance, his sister described him as a bottomless pit. He pushed his wavy gold and auburn locks from his dark blue eyes and licked his chops. His stomach growled at his imagination, making Avaleigh roll her shimmering sapphire irises. Her long sunkissed hair was tied back into a tail, which she readjusted as they walked. She wanted to be ready to face any monster that could attack them. Hayden; however, kept his nonchalant posture as he stepped lightly with his staff tucked behind his neck and his arms resting over it.

"Don't whistle so loud," Avaleigh said. "I don't want to have to fight monsters all the way to Colber."

"I don't think there are as many monsters in the wilds as they say," answered Hayden, his sly grin reflecting his smugness. "We are casters of an ancient bloodline. Monsters do not stand a chance against the two of us."

"You've never fought one before?" Avaleigh snarkily shot back. "What do you suppose will happen if our magic isn't powerful enough?"

"That's on you," Hayden shrugged. "I've been following your lead since I started training as a caster."

Avaleigh huffed at her brother's sarcasm, but knowing his words were not just teasing. Monsters of the wilds were the very reason cities and hamlets were walled up. Even farmland had to be barricaded with guards on duty. She looked around, seeing the open road with fields of grass and trees on either side. Birds were chirping and small squirrels were stomping about. If a monster threat were about, she assured herself no small animals would be so at ease.

The two walked for a time, each one looking behind them every so often to see Holprice beginning to fade in the distance. Still in the early morning, after they had traveled a half hour perhaps, Avaleigh noticed Hayden had ceased whistling and his pace had slowed. Her brother had taken notice of the birds ceasing in their delightful chirping, and squirrels were suddenly nowhere to be seen.

The grass in the distance rustled, and Hayden gripped his staff with one hand while electrical currents swirled around in the other. Avaleigh held tightly to her staff as she began rubbing her fingers together with the other, feeling air molecules coming together, being drawn to her, and generating a vapor mist at her feet. Hayden stepped behind her, remembering how they worked best together.

"No mercy," he whispered.

2

The Dread By the River

There is nothing quite like a young boy who has yet to taste the fear of survival. But Hayden must have missed such a lesson. Avaleigh could sense his blood pumping wildly, waiting for whatever would pop out of the high grass, which appeared tall enough to hide monsters waiting to pounce. Instead, what emerged was a bushy-tailed fox with a rabbit hanging from its mouth.

"Come on!" Hayden exclaimed. "I was so ready!"

Avaleigh laughed, but then quickly shushed her brother from continuing his rant of how he was about to lay waste to some "monster butt."

"That was a scream," she said. "I'm sure of it."

Both held their breath a bit to listen intently. The scream came again. Avaleigh and Hayden darted toward the sound, rounding a bend to take notice of a man doing his best to stay in a tree, and out of the snapping jaws of three common monsters known as Warptooths.

Known to inhabit all four kingdoms, Warptooths are four-legged canine creatures with protruding, sleek fur that is usually gray or mildly dark brown. A Warptooth has a great deal of speed but lacks the stamina to run long distances. They can be clever and are respectful hunters. Some are domesticated as pets, but most of them remain in packs out in the wilds.

"Do you suppose they're guarding the hamlet?" Avaleigh asked. "I'd hate to kill someone's pet."

"Then how are we going to keep them from eating that man who is dumb enough to climb up such a small tree?" Hayden replied.

Suddenly, a loud whistling came from the farmhouse in the distance from an elderly man. As he drew nearer, his voice held a raspy and grumpy tone.

"Told you to stay away from my property, you swindler," the old man shouted. The Warptooths had ceased being somewhat aggressive but kept their gaze on the man in the tree. "I told you that I don't need anything you're selling."

"I didn't even set foot on your property," the man in the tree exclaimed. "I was on my way to Holprice, and your vicious monsters attacked me."

"They don't attack unless provoked," the old man shot back. "Either your feet touched my ground or you're lying."

"What if he isn't lying?" Avaleigh piped up. The old man and his Warptooths whipped their heads about to face the children. "Warptooths can be very territorial, and even expand what they believe belongs to them. Could it be…?

"Who in blazes are you two?" The old man interjected.

"Casters from Holprice—duh," Avaleigh stepped arrogantly forward.

"You're the youngest casters I've ever seen outside those walls," the old man retorted. "You're either very brave or stupid to leave the safety of Holprice, or you've just got a death wish."

"We are powerful casters," Hayden puffed up. "We can handle anything Goolwind throws at us."

"Can you now, boy?" The old man scratched his chin. "Well, from what I know about casters, they help us plain folk with monster problems."

"You have a monster problem?" Hayden inquired.

"I do. This fella in the tree sold me a liquid scent to keep a monster from coming to eat my chickens. Don't have more than a handful left."

"That was before winter," the man in the tree exclaimed.

"Eh, the monster I'm dealing with hibernates, but it's already back," the old man spat. "Didn't take long for his belly to become full again with my new chickens I bought. The scent didn't work."

"What kind of monster is it?" Hayden asked.
"Scaley Dread," the old man lifted a fiendish smirk.

Found near rivers, lakes, and even in harsh marshlands, Scaley Dreads are dominate semi-aquatic reptiles that appear much like alligators or crocodiles. They range in all different sizes with the largest one ever recorded as fifty-two feet long, snout to tail. They are spotted creatures, made up of grays and blacks, with pointy scales armoring all along their backs.

SCALEY DREAD

"Must have eaten a lot of chickens then," Avaleigh said.

"Show us where it is then," Hayden pressed. "We could use the practice."

Avaleigh slapped him on the back of his head and shushed him. But Hayden wouldn't budge from what he set his mind to doing. He demanded the old man take them to the thing. As they followed him, who was still in disbelief about the two young casters, the old man said that maybe the two youngsters were exactly what he needed—as either, they would kill the Scaley Dread or it would eat them, giving the old man another day to try and figure out how to save his chickens.

The tracks of the monster were deep in the soil near the chicken coop strewn about with blood and feathers. It had once appeared quite large, built tremendously thorough in its design, but now shattered into splinters along the ground. The remaining chickens were surrounded only by a small wire cage. No doubt easy for a large monster to get through.

"We could use another chicken as bait to draw it out," Hayden suggested.

"No way," the old man retorted. "I've lost enough chickens already. If you want to fight the thing, follow its tracks to the river. I can't afford any more destruction on my property."

Avaleigh remained reluctant to follow the monster back to its resting place. Yet Hayden didn't want to appear like he was a coward, and he started stepping forward, tearing away from his sister's grasp on his shoulder. She could not let him wander off alone.

"Your foolishness is going to get us killed," she said to him.

"There's a Tremor of Power around here," Hayden replied. "Also, how will we ever become great casters if we don't face what others fear?"

"I stand corrected. Your stupidity is going to get us killed." Avaleigh huffed.

The river wasn't far, nor was the enormous Scaley Dread that lay next to it. Its head remained still, held up high toward the sun, with its massive, spotted body straightened fully out along the shoreline. The monster's mouth stayed agape showing off the feathers still stuck between its teeth.

"Tha-th-that's a good size," Hayden stuttered out in a whisper. "How big would you say that is?"

"Twenty, maybe thirty feet long," Avaleigh replied, keeping her voice hushed. "If I can douse it in water, can you electrify it?"

"I will give it all I got," Hayden answered.

"If it's not enough, then make a cyclone to keep it at bay."

Hayden nodded. Avaleigh began generating vapor around her. She crept the water along the ground until it settled right underneath the monster. A rushing spout of water flew up from beneath it, hurling it straight into the air. It landed flat on its back, soaked from Avaleigh's spell.

"Now Hayden!" She shouted.

The boy had mustered all the electrical power he could and shot it forth from his palm, reaching the soft underbelly of the Scaley Dread, making it growl in pain. The monster did not remain on its back for long, and rolled over, still in shock from Hayden's Thunder Strike. The boy began casting his Sinister Cyclone until he noticed the monster was staring right at him. In an instant, it darted toward him at an unexpected speed. Hayden was quick to respond, running away and dodging trees to escape its jaws. It ran by Avaleigh without even a glance. She hesitated, but soon took off after both, doing her best to concentrate on casting her Stormy Gale, in hopes of freezing and slowing the monster down.

Hayden knew he would not be able to outrun the Scaley Dread for long, but he managed to reach the clearing of the old man's farm. He turned to see the thing right on his heels, and he leaped just high enough as the monster's jaws snapped shut, continuing onward underneath him. Hayden's quick thinking kept him out of reach of the Scaley Dread's jaws, as he cast a Sinister Cyclone right underneath himself in mid-air. The cyclone formed instantly and shot Hayden even higher into the air. Though he was getting dizzy, he remained safely above the monster's reach for a time.

Avaleigh had caught up and cast her Stormy Gale spell with rain and frost upon the monster. The wind picked up speed and blew a layer of frost to slow the Scaley Dread's movement. Hayden landed with a tumbling thud as the cyclone dissipated, well away from the monster's reach. Still, the boy felt his breath slow and his vision darkened until he passed out.

Avaleigh kept up her Stormy Gale, noticing the monster slowly turning and taking notice of her. Its powerful legs dug deep into the ground, sluggishly pushing against the frost and wind beating against it. The young caster was beginning to tire, but she stood her ground, desperately wanting to freeze the thing completely.

However, her vision began to blur and she felt her head begin to feel weightless. But before she passed out, Avaleigh noticed the old man approach the monster with a pickaxe. It did not take notice of him as he plunged it into a vulnerable spot on the back of its skull. The Scaley Dread plopped down, lifeless. Suddenly, she felt her legs give way.

The two young casters awoke inside the man's home, each covered with a blanket, and next to a crackling fireplace. The old man sat in a chair across from them, whittling away at a piece of wood, doing mostly what older men do to pass the time.

"You two got guts. I'll give you that!" The old man said, taking notice that Avaleigh's eyes were open. "I've been doing what I can to kill that thing for well over a year now. Not sure where it came from or how it got there. But it's gone now."

"Why didn't you send word to Holprice of your need?" Avaleigh asked.

"Ah, they don't need to spend time on me," the old man replied. "I'm grateful for you two helping me though. I'll make sure Holprice knows about what you've done."

"We'd appreciate it if you didn't," Hayden chimed in, getting a scrunched and confused look from the old man.

"What he means is that we were told to keep a low profile," Avaleigh quickly said. "Our mission is secretive, but we were told to try and not fight monsters along the way."

"Along the way to where?" The old man had grown suspicious.

"To Dundlen," Hayden interjected. "We're on our way to Dundlen."

"Are you now?" The old man nodded. "Nothing of my affair, but hopefully you don't run into anything more powerful than a Scaley Dread on your way."

"We can handle Warptooths just fine," Hayden replied. "Plus, if we stick to the road, that should be the only thing that bothers us, really."

"I see," the old man smiled. "Well, if you're set on traveling to Dundlen, you should know there's a couple of forests you'll have to travel through, none of which hold just Warptooths but much more powerful monsters along the way...or you should just run along home where you belong."

"We cannot, sir," Avaleigh jumped to her feet. "Our mission is clear. Don't make us threaten you by endangering what we have set out to do."

"Keep your threats," the old man said. "You are not the first young stubborn casters to set out into the world to prove themselves."

"We're not trying to prove ourselves," Hayden joined his sister in standing up. "We're looking for answers."

"To what?" The old man chuckled.

"That we cannot say," Avaleigh said.

"I understand," the old man replied. "At least let me assist you to get where you want to go, but also let me give you some advice. Wherever you are going, get much stronger before you get there. You both show great promise, but lack technique in channeling your strength."

"And how would you know that," Avaleigh sneered.

"I was once an ambitious caster, myself," the old man admitted. He rose from his seat and walked over to the mantle above the fireplace. He unhooked two silver amulet necklaces and held them out to the young casters. "Here, these will help you channel your magical strength until you learn how to do it without them."

Avaleigh and Hayden graciously took them, noticing the old man grin for a moment before he turned his back.

"If you leave now, I can say I never saw you leave," he said. "There's still plenty of daylight to make it to Tolin. Just follow the main road. Make sure you get there before sundown. Nightfall is a nightmare in the wilds."

3
Tolin

ayden led the way to the first Tremor of Power as Avaleigh and he stepped lightly out of the old man's lodgings. He had sensed it down by the river while Avaleigh had sensed one in the opposite direction. The two young casters hurried back to the river where they both paused to take precautions that no other monsters lay in wait, especially another Scaley Dread. Though Hayden had sensed it, Avaleigh spotted the tremor first and pointed it out to him.

"You go ahead," she said. "You felt this one first. I'll take the next one."

While little is known about a Tremor of Power's appearance, even less is known about what it feels like to receive its surge into one's body. However, this one appeared more like a wave of wind, dancing in a circular motion with a slight golden hue as rays of sunshine danced through it ever so tenderly. Hayden's hand reached out, and without an incantation or special spell casting, the boy soaked his arm in its strength until it absorbed into him—nothing more than a heavy sigh came from him once the power became his own. When Hayden opened his eyes, Avaleigh saw his pupils ignite with a bright light for a time and then fade back to their normal state.

"I never get tired of that," Hayden smiled. "It's so warm in my tummy."

"We need to get moving," Avaleigh said, returning his friendly demeanor. "I'll race you to the next one!"

The two young casters made their way back up the hill and to the old man's farm. They did not bother speaking to him, as he was out on his back porch whittling away again. He didn't look up from his work, though Avaleigh did see a grin appear across his face as they raced by.

The other Tremor of Power was located within the grounds of a bare wheat field, some distance beyond the shattered chicken coop, near the corner of the property's defense wall—made of stone like many, but one, in particular, appeared to be out of place. The stone lay at the bottom of the pile with the same wave-like wind swaying in midair. The hue was no different either, and Avaleigh stepped forward, placing her hand in the middle of the wave. Her eyes shut but her mind did not remain peaceful.

A vision galloped through her soul, a place she had never seen before. An army marched against its fortress gates, and for a moment, she could not catch her breath. She felt Hayden's hands grab hold, shaking her from the vision.

"What's the matter?!" He cried.

"Nothing," Avaleigh regained her senses. "This one came with a vision."

"That's strange," Hayden sighed. "What was it?"

"Armies marching against a fortress I've never seen before," she replied. "I'm not sure what to make of it."

Hayden shrugged and began walking toward the main road. Avaleigh realized she had dropped her staff when the vision pulsed through her. She still felt shaken but did not admit it to Hayden. A vision had never come with a Tremor of Power before, and it was one so strong she had felt wisped away by the reality presented to her. But she knew no time could be given to wrestle with it for now. She picked up her staff and hurried to catch up with her brother.

The town of Tolin did not stand far from Holprice—just to the southwest, with mostly wide-open and fertile rolling hills, and tall grasslands with a few trees sprinkled along the way. Avaleigh and Hayden found shade beneath one of them from the unusually scorching spring day. They were enjoying a quick bite to eat, slightly off the road when Avaleigh began hearing voices conversing in the distance, drawing closer and closer. She knew instantly the voices belonged to no humans.

They were Goblins, likely of the tribe to the northeast of Holprice— mountain and forest dwellers, stout and fattened through trade with the towns to the south. She could tell by the way they were dressed in fine clothes and shiny armor. Yet their green pointy ears and wide scrunched noses still

GOBLIN

made them hideous in her mind. She had seen their kind before, as Goblins from the tribe often stopped to trade in the city. But most people in Holprice didn't seem to care for their wares. Normally, she would pass on by them without a word, that is if her brother was not feeling especially cheeky. And today, Hayden couldn't keep his mouth shut.

"I do believe I see a Goblin, a hobblin, and a wobblin over next to me," Hayden called out. "With a nose so widely stretched, what will they think of next?"

This was no form of gibberish insult. Hayden had just instigated a game of sorts that no one truly knows how it started. One thing is for sure when addressing a Goblin's walk, weight, or nose, it means game on. No Goblin could resist prattling a retort. It became one of Hayden's hobbies, watching these kinds of competitions, yet he had never competed.

"I do believe I see…a boy, with a stick toy, unable to enjoy, beneath the off-road tree," a bulky and stout Goblin, bigger than the others who followed him, stepped lively toward the young casters. His green skin appeared as a hue almost black, and sweat trickled down his brow. "With hair so gold, but not so old, he sleeps with mommy each night to be consoled."

"I'm putting an end to this!" Avaleigh sighed heavily and slapped Hayden on his shoulder. "We don't have time for this."

"What? Too afraid to let him finish what he started, love?" The Goblin mocked, and lifted his snout into the air.

"How about this," Hayden ignored his sister. "If I win, I get to select anything from your satchel."

"And if I win, I get everything you own," the Goblin sneered, now surrounded by the others, outnumbering the young casters ten to one. "I'll even take your clothes and your little woman from you. Maybe we get a good price from the Gnolls."

"Enough!" Avaleigh leaped to her feet. The rest of the Goblins jumped back seeing water vapor begin to swirl around her.

"Oh come on, love. That's cheating," the Goblin pointed out. "I'm just trying to get into his head to mess him up so I can win. We don't deal in slavery."

"At least not anymore," another Goblin spoke up with a whimper. The head Goblin turned to him with a wide-eyed glare that made the smaller one clamp his jaw shut.

"Come on, caster," the head Goblin reasoned. "Just put away the magic. We get it. You're very scary. But at least let us finish the game. I thought it fortunate to get in some practice for the competition in Lem."

"You're trying to reach Lem?" Hayden interjected, knowing Lem was on the way to Colber. "We are also on our way there, hoping to visit the monastery over in Shroe."

"No doubt you'd have to travel through Lem to get there," the Goblin answered. "We've had a long journey already, and we're hoping to spend a night in Tolin. Having a couple of casters along wouldn't be so bad. You could help keep the Warptooths off us. There always seems to be a pack roaming around between Tolin and Lem. What do you say?"

"What competition in Lem?" Avaleigh had lowered her staff.

"I don't suspect casters take much of a fancy to such things," the Goblin replied. "But Lem has a great insult competition each year. The winner gets a pretty decent-sized purse. This year, rumor has it, there's something else placed in the pot, something a caster might like. Could be a spell of sorts."

"What would you do with a spell?" Avaleigh asked.

"I'd sell if of course," the Goblin laughed. "Holprice monastery usually pays pretty well for old books and things like that should we come across them."

"What if it's the book?" Hayden whispered to Avaleigh. "We need to check it out."

Avaleigh stared for a moment at her brother, and then her eyes turned toward the Goblins.

"I think traveling together would be wise," she admitted.

"We already had a run-in with a Scaley Dread," Hayden blurted out.

"...And here you are," the Goblin appeared impressed. "The name's Grug."

"My name is Ha..." Avaleigh swiftly kicked the back of her brother's leg. "Lo! My name is Halo."

"My name is Glenna," Avaleigh said.

"Well, Halo and Glenna. We best get moving before the sun gets too low. Tolin shouldn't be long now."

Twilight glazed over the landscape as the young casters and Goblin crew waltzed into Tolin. Nothing appeared exceptional about the town—no tall structures or monuments, just simple wood and brick buildings blowing smoke into the evening sky. Farmland and cottages surrounded the town and were intertwined within its defense walls, with crops of wheat, tomatoes, and grapes growing right up to the lodgings for travelers and various other shops. Each one held a unique sign to display over its door, making it easy to depict the establishment.

No eye held its gaze to their entry to Tolin, except for some friendly passers-by. Grug suggested they find a place to settle for the night, the place with the best mutton, which is a tasty morsel of sheep leg.

"How do we do that?" Avaleigh asked.

"It's easy," Grug replied snickering. "I already know."

Avaleigh chuckled at Grug's reply. She and Hayden followed the Goblin crew to a lodging just on the other side of town that held a warmer welcome with an elegantly whittled sign above the door. The innkeeper was a middle-aged woman, passive-aggressively persuading her husband to stoke the fires and get mutton on the grill while she showed the guests to their rooms. Her husband leisurely dragged his feet around to the two fireplaces in the main hall. He proceeded to step outside where a large fire pit was dug out with hot coals and an iron rack hanging just above it. He stoked the coals to a blaze, adding more wood, and laid large portions of greasy meat upon it.

Hayden, of course, was the first to exit the room that he shared with his sister on the second floor when the alluring scent of fresh mutton swayed throughout the hall. He peeked over the banister and saw the meat-covered bones steaming on one of the large tables. Next to it were fire-roasted tomatoes, freshly picked grapes, and hot cider waiting. He had already sunk his teeth into a bit of everything, including alternating between two mutton chops when the Goblins took their seats at the tables.

The Goblins' table manners were no better, scarfing through one entire platter in a matter of minutes. Soon the innkeeper's husband had another platter of mutton ready. And soon another, but all were gone in a matter of minutes.

"You don't need to eat with the likes of them," Avaleigh heard an old woman's voice behind her.

The innkeeper had offered to draw her a hot bath before dinner, and Avaleigh never turned down a chance to be pampered. The innkeeper had brought her a plate of food, and set it down on a small table beside the tub, resting near another roaring fireplace. The hospitable elderly woman took another heated pot of water away from the fire and poured it into the tub.

"There we go," she said. "I figured you'd want to soak a little longer. However, the meat is going fast. So, I brought you a plate."

"Thank you very much," Avaleigh smiled. "I've never been to Tolin before. I've spent most of my life in Holprice."

"O' that is a lovely place," the innkeeper chatted away. "Are you a caster perchance?"

"I am," Avaleigh admitted.

"Well," the innkeeper stooped down and placed her arm along the tub rim. "Tolin appears like a simple place, but we've got some interesting things to be found in our shops, some things could pique a caster's interest."

"If hot baths and warm beds are your idea of simple, then I shall certainly like Tolin all the more," Avaleigh replied, sharing a chuckle with the innkeeper.

"You have a good night, deary," the innkeeper said as she began to exit the room. "But let me know if you need anything else."

Silence filled the room once more and Avaleigh leaned her head back hearing nothing but the crackling of the fire. Her thoughts, however, broke through the comforts of the evening. What had suddenly struck her mind was the realization that she, in fact, had never been to Tolin, nor anywhere else for that matter. She began to feel sick for home.

Holprice did not hold the simplicity she now encountered, but it was all she had known. Her home held a tall cathedral monastery, and most of the residential buildings reflected the pointy architecture of its steeples, which often overwhelmed her senses. She enjoyed getting away from the gloomy stone and narrow streets to her father's study, where she could create worlds in her mind by reading through historical manuscripts of ancient and forgotten times. In another passing moment, she realized she missed something of beauty her home always presented each early spring—the blooming of almond trees. The blossoms made the city bright. At times, the trees began to bloom when snow still glittered all over including the farmland surrounding the monastery, and the nut groves appeared like a white canvas painted of bright colors from the tall towers of the monastery. To catch a glimpse of the sight, one had to be swift as the day began and the markets filled with people bustling to muddy the white and ignore the blossoms singing out to the sun. Time is money in Holprice. And for many casters, time spent doing nothing means time wasted.

Her father taught her the opposite, however, believing priceless moments to be found in the silent beats of the day, the times when nothing alarms or distracts. Becoming a great caster meant listening more and speaking less. She felt he was a mystic among sheep, and he wasn't even born from their bloodline. He married into it.

Avaleigh believed that's why her mother fell in love with her father—his introspectiveness, his willingness to learn, and his fearlessness of desiring to be comfortable with the unknown. Avaleigh took his lessons to heart, and during the silent times, that's when she knew she missed him the most. The beauty of Holprice reminded her of her father, while the simplicity of Tolin did as well. For that, she was glad. She washed the tears from her eyes, wrapped a towel around herself, and got dressed. Hayden had already climbed into bed and snored away when she slid into the warm bed next to his.

"Father also snores like that," she smiled.

4
No Pants, No Problem

Morning came to Tolin with the unpleasant sounds of distant shouting. At first, Avaleigh awoke, startled, believing that the screams were a part of her dream. She took a deep breath and sat up, only to hear more clamor outside. She leaped out of bed seeing Hayden still deep in slumber, his mouth agape with drool flowing down his pillow.

The young caster shot her brother a disgusted look and quietly exited the room. She made her way swiftly down the steps, not seeing the innkeeper or her husband anywhere. Obliviously, she opened the front door and stepped out into the early morning light. She listened again, hearing the shouting echo loudly just down the town's main path. Avaleigh hurried, with staff in hand, to find the commotion. Immense chaos had shattered shop stalls, and Grug and his Goblin crew were assisting the town guard against what looked like a raiding party of another Goblin tribe riding Brutal Swine.

Brutal Swine are wild boars that can grow to great size. They are made up of a variety of hues between black and light brown, but more commonly are more toward the lighter side. Some may even be spotted with black spread along their bristle-like fur. The beasts' tusks and horns do not cease growing throughout their lifetime, and their hooves are razor-sharp. Brutal Swine are known to be extremely aggressive, unintelligent, and not above charging anything remotely appearing smaller than itself—including little girls who are standing unaware and surveying the scene.

BRUTAL SWINE

Avaleigh was quick to evade the Brutal Swine's charge and barely escaped the Goblin's swiping club as well. Water vapor already surrounded her when she rolled to her feet. It accumulated faster as the dew of the morning had not yet dried and joined the swirling vapor. She blasted a Crashing Tide spell into the Brutal Swine sending it flying backward as it turned back around and began charging her again. Its rider tumbled hard along the ground and did not return to its feet as Grug brought a throwing axe down to meet the Goblin's skull. The large blackish-green Goblin then pulled it out and heaved it at the Brutal Swine that was still trying to find its footing. The blade of the axe landed but only appeared to make the Brutal Swine more enraged.

"Come at me then!" Grug shouted.

A sudden icy gust of wind slowed the Brutal Swine's pace, which allowed Grug to topple the beast with another axe throw, sinking the blade into one of its leg joints. The beast made a thud when it hit the ground, and its heart was suddenly pierced by the spears of two other Goblins in Grug's crew.

The town guard allied with Grug's Goblins and began making progress against the invaders, taking down another enemy Goblin with arrows while their Goblin allies punctured holes into the swine steed. Avaleigh manifested a greater Crashing Tide as four more invaders were riding toward the town guard. They were cast aside like rag dolls and soon dispatched as they lay stunned.

A strike of lightning came and hit one of the town guardsmen. He immediately fell to his knees, crying out, but remained alive. Avaleigh looked about to try and find her brother, to scold him over his inaccuracy. But Hayden was nowhere in sight. Instead, one of the invading Goblins held up a small staff with a violet, glowing rock shard attached to the head.

"Since when do Goblins know how to cast?" Avaleigh thought. She turned to Grug who appeared just as bewildered.

The other invading Goblins had ceased their advance, allowing the Goblin caster to move forward, taunting the young girl to come out in the open and meet it. The Goblin caster sat upright on its Brutal Swine steed, an alpha swine that was twice the size of the others. Avaleigh stepped forward, accepting the challenge.

"He can't cast on his own," the girl heard Grug call to her. "Destroy the stone to destroy his power."

Avaleigh considered his words, but she held to a different idea. She wanted to take the Goblin's stone to study it for herself. It could be, perhaps, a quicker way to learn Hayden's Thunder Strike Tempest spell. Or at the very least, it could be a way for Hayden to increase his power.

The girl did her best to hold her composure amid her adversary. She felt cold sweat upon her brow, and her heart thumped violently in her chest. She knew that she needed to calm her nerves, but this was only the second large beast she would fight. Her mind raced with fearful thoughts telling her that she wasn't ready.

Without hesitation, the Goblin sank its heels into the Brutal Swine making the beast squeal and begin to charge, brandishing its large tusks. Avaleigh covered her ears, frozen in the moment, she knew her life was about to come to an end. Her eyes suddenly caught sight of an axe that landed very near the charging swine, halting the Goblin's charge. It was Grug, stepping lively out and growling something in an unknown tongue.

The other raiding Goblins began growling with Grug. The Goblin holding the Thunder Strike staff turned its head about and then dismounted its beast. Avaleigh appeared baffled for a moment until Grug uttered to her.

"I called him a coward for not dueling you without his swine," Grug said. "His brethren agreed. So, he will face you now without his steed."

"Thank you," Avaleigh sighed.

"Just don't freeze up again," Grug said. "I can't help you anymore."

Avaleigh nodded and turned her gaze back toward the Goblin, who had shooed his steed away from him. The young girl and her Goblin adversary were surrounded by a weathered pasture fence and piles of scattered hay bales. Avaleigh made use of one of the hay bale piles as the Goblin struck first, zapping a tremendous bolt her way. She ducked behind the pile, but the shock blew the whole thing apart. However, she was left unharmed. Avaleigh took the opportunity to send a Stormy Gale back toward the Goblin, blowing all the hay pieces with it.

The Goblin tried to maneuver away from the hay dust, but his sight became clouded, and when it settled, Avaleigh was nowhere to be seen. The Goblin turned back to his tribe of raiders, but they only stared at him. None revealed to him any clues of where the girl had gone. He grunted and peered menacingly through his helm at the several hay bale piles throughout the field.

What appeared like a good strategy, also masked Avaleigh's fear. She knew she would not be fast enough to dodge the Goblin's Thunder Strike. Taking the Goblin head-on would be suicide if she tried to cast again. From where Grug stood, he could see Avaleigh from the corner of his eye, noticing she was struggling to muster her courage. Suddenly, he felt a small tug on his cloak. Grug turned to see Hayden, with unbrushed hair and only half-dressed.

"Where's your pants boy?" Grug asked, confused.

"You're lucky I'm wearing underwear," Hayden replied. "Which one of you snot-nosed critters nabbed my pants from me last nigh…?"

The boy had suddenly noticed the duel taking place. Grug wrapped the boy with one arm to keep him from charging out to help his sister.

"You don't let go of me right now," Hayden spat. "I will fry you and every Goblin within a hundred miles of here."

"I know this looks grim," Grug replied. "But Glenna is doing great. She's outsmarted the lug."

"Is that Goblin casting?" Hayden wiggled even harder. "Goblins can't cast!"

"This one can," Grug said. "He has some type of caster stone."

"A what!?" Hayden resounded.

"A caster stone," Grug hushed. "It is infused with the power of a Tempest spell."

"My spell!" Hayden continued shouting, seeing the Goblin light up a hay bale pile that didn't reveal Avaleigh's hiding place. The Goblin caster stomped his feet and continued to ignite another.

The boy became so furious that lightning lit up around his body and shocked Grug to the ground. The Goblin remained stunned for a moment, just long enough to watch Hayden dart out to the duel. The Goblin caster took notice of him and growled, something perhaps in the Goblin tongue that bellowed his displeasure of another challenger on the field. The stone in his staff glowed brightly and began to surge even brighter as the Goblin powered up to attack the boy.

Hayden planted his feet, his pupils holding a wild countenance, and his heartbeat earnestly like a predator waiting for the right moment to pounce. When the lightning flew out from the Goblin's staff, Hayden received the Thunder Strike, almost as if someone had just passed him a ball—and in the same motion, spun the Goblin's electric currents around, added his own to it, and shot it back in the Goblin's direction. The Goblin's staff exploded, just like lightning striking a tree. The stone tumbled into the dirt while the sizzling Goblin caster lay flat on its back. He began trembling and tried to find his footing once again, but fell upon his back again. He frantically peeled off his armor from his scorched flesh and then cried out as he removed his helm.

"Thunder Strike is my bread and butter!" Hayden yelled. "Be thankful I didn't use all my strength."

Avaleigh came out from hiding, seeing that the rest of the Goblin raiders were beginning to scatter. Grug had joined her side, but Avaleigh was staring at her brother, amazed at the power he had just displayed.

"How did you reverse that spell?" She gawked. "Where did you learn that?"

"I dreamt it," Hayden replied. "I think it was that Tremor of Power. I knew something weird needed to happen cause yesterday I didn't really feel anything when I absorbed it."

"Tremor of Power?" Grug asked. "You are casters of the ancient bloodline?"

"Something like that," Avaleigh admitted, not wanting to divulge more than her brother already foolishly had.

"Then your names are not Glenna nor Halo," Grug scowled. "I do not like being lied to. I know your uncle fairly well—Avaleigh and Hayden. What do you suppose he would do if he knew you were out here?"

"Probably shut us in our rooms," Avaleigh sighed.

"After asking us how it was," Hayden jokingly added.

"I must see you safely back to Holprice," Grug said.

"No!" The young casters shouted.

"I cannot allow you to travel any further," Grug reasoned. "It's too dangerous."

"You felt my sting," Hayden gritted his teeth. "If you try to take us back, I'll make sure you and your Goblin friends end up like that fried egg over there."

Hayden pointed toward the Goblin caster who still tried to find his footing. Grug stared into the young boy's eyes and then began to laugh. He stepped lively, passed the two young casters, and removed the Goblin caster's head from his shoulders with one swing of his axe before the young casters could turn away, which made them both flinch.

"If you think this is dangerous," Grug explained. "Then you have no idea what awaits you, wherever you wish to go in this world."

Hayden walked over to where the Goblin's casting stone lay. He scooped it up with his hand, feeling a slight surge of energy dance through his veins.

"I wonder if we can find more of these," Hayden wondered aloud to his sister. "I can feel a slight increase…in something…within me."

"I thought you might," Avaleigh said. "You'll have to teach me how to reverse that Thunder Strike spell so I won't have to hide behind hay bales."

Hayden laughed and turned to Grug, who was standing confused at what was taking place.

"Listen here, Grug," Avaleigh bravely spoke. "We have business in Colber. That we can be honest about. You take us safely to Colber, and if we don't find what we're looking for, then you can escort us back to Holprice on your way back home. But we must reach Colber." Grug huffed as the other Goblins of his band joined them.

"I don't think I have much of a choice," he said. "If it helps you gain knowledge in casting, then your uncle won't beat me up too badly."

"Here's your pants, Master Hayden," one of the Goblins held out the boy's trousers. "It was just good fun."

"I know," Hayden smiled. "I don't mind a good prank. Now give them here. My legs are freezing."

5
Night Troubles

The path to Lem would take about a five-day trek, over rolling grassland hills and wildflowers. The mountains of Shroe lay solemnly in the west, and Hayden took notice of a narrow trail leading toward them when they reached a small crossroads.

"We could skip Lem and go straight over the mountains to Shroe," Hayden suggested.

"No one takes the mountain pass, boy," Grug grunted. "You need to learn about monsters a lot more before you travel unknown roads."

"Monsters don't frighten me," Hayden scoffed. "You saw how I took care of that Goblin back there, and Avaleigh and I took care of a Scaley Dread before we met you."

"Barely," Avaleigh added.

"Luck is good to have on your side," Grug replied. "That Goblin was nothing but a trickster. And I suppose your Scaley Dread was an adolescent."

"What do you mean, adolescent?" Hayden shot back. "The thing was over twenty feet long!"

"Then he still had a long way to grow," Grug grinned. "Scaley Dread adolescents are not very clever, and are easily fooled."

"I made it mad!" Hayden argued. "I shocked it immensely and it charged us!"

"A smart one would have laid still, making you believe it was dead," Grug patiently retorted. "Then when you approached it, the thing would have struck."
"Even still…" Hayden began.

"Stop this!" Avaleigh shouted. "For once, would you listen? We don't know these lands nor the monsters. All we know is what we've learned from books."

"At least I didn't cower behind a pile of hay," Hayden shot back, showing that his pride had been pricked.

"How dare you!" Avaleigh's face became engulfed in bright red. "I was trying to stay alive."

"Maybe, you're not powerful enough for the outside world," Hayden sneered.

"How about we find out!" Avaleigh began gathering water vapor around her, and Hayden gritted his teeth beginning to summon lightning into his fist.

Both were suddenly knocked off their feet, falling harshly to the ground. Their arms were swiftly held tightly behind their backs and daggers placed against their throats.

"A valuable lesson to both of you," Grug began, seeing his Goblin followers clinching the children securely. "Fighting amongst yourselves will only get you killed out here. You were just ambushed by a bunch of Goblin merchants. If it were any other Goblin tribe, I'd say your throats would be cut by now."

"I'm going to fry all of you," Hayden spat.

Grug's large hand grasped a hold of the boy's throat, squeezing it just enough to make Hayden gag.

"I've had enough of your disrespect, boy," Grug growled. "I owe you for shocking me before. But you should understand, I know how to keep a caster from casting—cut off his hands."

"Stop!" Avaleigh whimpered. "This is not the way."

Grug sighed, knowing his anger was getting the better of him. The boy was stubborn and ignorant, but he knew Avaleigh to be right. He leaned in close to Hayden, the boy's eyes tearing up with anger and fear.

"You think your Thunder Strike will win you every battle?" Grug whispered. Hayden didn't respond. "Up in those mountains, boy, there is a monster impervious to lightning—one, maybe more. Do you know what a Blighttalon is, boy?

"Blighttalons can be found throughout the four kingdoms and are birds of prey, most closely related to eagles, but on a much larger scale. They are rare and carry the ability to cast Sinister Cyclone with the flap of their wings. They are mostly white with black streaks running through their feathers,

BLIGHTTALON

with black talons and beaks. Their favorite prey is Brutal Swine but are not above swooping down from the skies to sink their talons into a Scaley Dread, and they are immune to electrical currents. Their wingspan is approximately twenty-four to thirty feet, and luckily do not appear to see humans as much of a meal worth their effort. However, they are highly protective of their nest, making them aggressively territorial," Avaleigh replied, channeling her memory from texts she previously studied.

Grug and the rest of the Goblins turned their heads slowly to the young girl, impressed by her memory, followed by their jaws growing agape.

"I like birds," Avaleigh shrugged.

The Goblins let the children go, and Avaleigh approached her brother, throwing her arms around him.

"I'm sorry," she said. "I don't want to fight you. I don't care if you're more powerful than me."

"Good," he replied, with a sniffle. "Cause I am."

"He's had a difficult time making friends," Avaleigh told Grug as they continued onward. Hayden was far in front with a couple of other Goblins staying slightly behind him. "Ever since his best friend betrayed him—not just betrayed him, but physically overpowered him—he's always felt like he has to prove his strength."

"I am not sure what that is like," Grug admitted. "I have always been strong. Regrettably, I have not always been reasonable the way you are. I am old enough to know now there is strength in both."

"He's obsessed with showing everyone he's not weak," Avaleigh continued. "I see that he is angry, still holding to the shame of losing when he believes he's supposed to be the best."

"Ambition is good," Grug replied. "Ignorance is not. Ambition keeps the mind teachable, while ignorance blinds one to their downfall. This is a philosophy I learned from your uncle."

"Hayden has yet to learn that lesson," Avaleigh confessed. "I too am learning such things. I wanted so badly to take power for myself, to become stronger. But when I dueled that Goblin caster, I realized I was not good enough."

"I thought you had a wonderful strategy," Grug said. "Before your brother came, I truly thought you were going to ambush him."

"I froze," Avaleigh sighed, heavily. "Hayden appears to carry all the confidence in his abilities…"

"…And you carry practicality, despite your racing emotions," Grug interjected. "Your confidence will grow in time. Being overconfident is ignorance, and often leads to disaster."

"I like talking to you, Grug," Avaleigh smiled. "I've never spoken philosophy with a Goblin before."

"Thank you, Miss Avaleigh," Grug replied, returning her smile. "I like talking to you too."

Midday came and went without incident of danger. Hayden had calmed himself, rejoining his sister's side. He began to joke around as if the events of that morning never happened. It seemed Grug also wished to forget as he challenged Hayden to another game of insults.

"Little boy, little boy, who else can you annoy? Your bum is oddly shaped like your face, and your breath is such a disgrace."

"O' Goblin, Goblin, won't you stop your wobblin? Your face is such a bore, and don't you know you smell like an old…"

"Hayden!" Avaleigh interjected. "Don't finish that!"

"What?" Hayden asked. "What's wrong with 'reservoir?' The old one in Holprice smells like vegetable farts."

Grug laughed.

Then a howling broke the pleasantries. The Goblins encircled, back-to-back with Grug, Avaleigh, and Hayden in the middle.

"That doesn't sound like a Warptooth," Avaleigh pointed out.

"It's not," Grug agreed. "That's a Savage Howler."

Savage Howlers are large, lone canines. They are aggressive beasts, with long fangs, and extremely sharp claws, and are excellent hunters. They despise most other canine creatures and do not often pass up a chance to run one down to kill it. They are also scavengers but prefer to hunt large prey, even large livestock.

SAVAGE HOWLER

Their fur is grayish in tone but often has golden streaks running up and down like pinstripes. Known for their vicious killing of other animals, Savage Howlers give off a loud howl once they've made a kill almost as if they're boasting about what they've done.

Again, the howling commenced. Grug surmised it was calling out to announce it had killed its prey, warning all to stay away. The troop began to move cautiously onward, keeping their eyes open, and remained silent as they went. While Savage Howlers usually didn't have an eye for Goblin meat, Grug knew they were not above attacking humans. Traveling with ones so young could make the beast bold enough to try and nab one of them.

"Stay close," Grug whispered. "It will be dark soon, and we don't need to lose sight of anyone with a Savage Howler around."

Hayden didn't appear so brave to fight. The howling of the beast was eerie and carried a melancholy tone, almost in a magical sense. He was also feeling weary from walking all day. Grug pointed out that is when the beast would likely strike when one is no longer paying attention. But what concerned Grug more was finding a haven for the night.

Just a ways up the road laid a small hamlet, where Grug and his companions usually spent the night in their previous travels, before continuing to Lem. The longest trek would come tomorrow, three days in the wilds, facing whatever monster during the day, and possibly Bonecrackles at night—skeletons that rise from the earth during the hours of darkness. Some can even be cursed undead with the ability to cast.

When they reached the hamlet, the buildings were still smoking from being set ablaze. They saw arrows and spears scattered throughout the hamlet, coupled with dead bodies strewn about, pierced by one or the other.

"This must be part of the same Goblin tribe that attacked Tolin," Grug said. "I wonder what has stirred them up."

"What do we do?" Avaleigh asked.

"We can't rest here," Grug replied. "Lem is in danger as it is closest to the tribe's home."

"What of Tolin?" Hayden asked.

"Tolin will send word to Holprice of what occurred," Grug reassured. "But I'm not sure if Lem knows of this, or even if Lem has been attacked at all."

"We should go then," Avaleigh said.

Grug nodded. The Goblins and the two young casters quickened their pace to leave the area, under Hayden's silent protest, as he longed to lay his head down to rest somewhere. They were no more than twenty paces away from the hamlet when Avaleigh caught the sound of bones tapping together. Grug was already staring at them, with his axes in hand. The other Goblins formed a line, as several more bones rose from the ground to form perfect humanoid skeletons with nothing but sharp fingers that they bared like claws. One, in particular, held the staff of a caster. It was covered with a tattered cloak—its eye sockets glowed fiercely red, and it let out a horrible screech that started the other bones to march toward the Goblins' line.

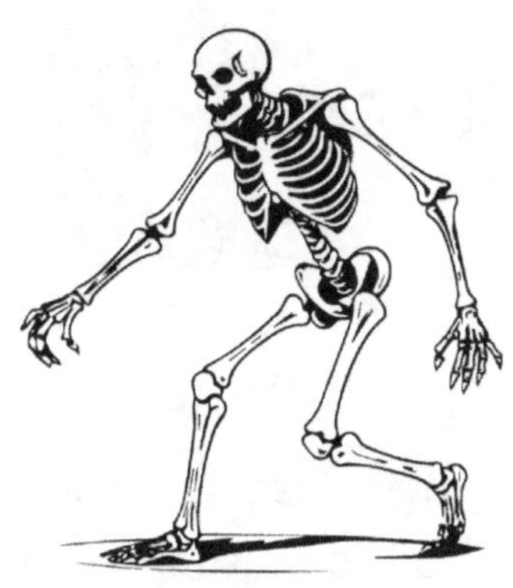

BONECRACKLE

BONECRACKLE CASTER

6

Homgrid's Curse

The Bonecrackles quickly dispersed their lines to flank and surround them. Hayden noticed it difficult to muster any of his strength to focus and cast a proficient spell.

"I'm so tired Avaleigh," he said to his sister.

"You best find your second wind, boy," Grug replied. "This is not the time to fall asleep."

The Goblin leader took notice of Avaleigh drawing water vapor to herself. A gust of chilling winds began swirling around her, and the droplets of water became hardened shards of ice.

"I suggest you all duck," she said.

As soon as the Goblins and Hayden crouched down, she erupted hundreds of shards in every direction. Every Bonecrackle surrounding them was hit and knocked backward to the ground— some even shattering from the impact of Avaleigh's casting.

Their fortunate first strike, however, became short-lived as, in another moment, a cluster of small cyclones barreled through them.

The young casters and the Goblins were hurled in every direction. Grug was the first to his feet, seeing that the Bonecrackle holding the staff had elevated above the ground, and began mustering a much larger Sinister Cyclone spell.

"So that's what that feels like," Hayden wobbled to his feet. He and two other Goblins had landed relatively in the same area, who also swiftly found their footing and rushed to his side. Many of the Bonecrackles were starting to put themselves back together, at least the ones that didn't have their bones shattered from the shards of ice hurled through them.

More Goblins found their footing and didn't waste any more time bashing the skulls of the Bonecrackles to cinders as they were still strewn along the soil—a logical conclusion of how to kill something already dead.

A strike of lightning grasped the Bonecrackle caster's attention. Hayden's aim missed the mark, but he had performed what he wished in drawing the glowing red eyes in his direction. The Bonecrackle caster brought its staff forward in the boy's direction, releasing the Sinister Cyclone spell it had been concocting. Grug took the opportunity to hurl one of his axes and it broke through the Bonecrackle caster's skull, sending it to fall to the ground, its bones scattering upon impact. Its Sinister Cyclone cast swiftly dissipated before reaching Hayden who knew he was helpless to defend against it. Yet nothing more than a stiff breeze shot through his hair and shoved him to his backside. The Goblins near him felt the impact as well, though much heavier than the boy, were able to plant their feet to not fall. They helped Hayden to his feet once more.

"That was fortunate," Grug said, seeing the other Bonecrackles had fallen in piles of bone heaps.

"What do you mean?" Avaleigh asked, seeing the others gathering around.

"I guess that would be your first encounter with a Bonecrackle caster," Grug assumed. "I've only come across them once before. We didn't have casters with us then, and several Goblins died that day."

"Was it controlling the other Bonecrackles?" Avaleigh continued to inquire.

"Most likely," Grug said. "It is believed Bonecrackles are a wandering curse, cast by Witches of the Wilds long ago. They liked to curse things, even casters they killed."

"Look," Hayden pointed out to his sister. "Do you see that—where the Bonecrackle caster landed?"

Avaleigh peered into the dim light of the night, but she could see a glowing, circular, and wavy light rising from the ground where the Bonecrackle caster had fallen. Grug and the other Goblins looked on puzzled as the two youngsters made their way to it. Hayden noticed a slight surge of green and shimmering gold drifting up and down the wavelengths.

"You take this one," he said to Avaleigh. "If it has a vision accompanying it, I don't want a disturbing image in my head at this hour."

Avaleigh grinned and reached out her hand. She noticed the Tremor of Power rising from the broken skull. And as her hand touched the tremor, she felt her body tense. Her mind focused on the sounds of mourning and when she opened her eyes, she saw apparitions of what befell the Bonecrackle caster.

"This wasn't the work of a Witch of the Wilds," she said. "He was the caster of this hamlet. The Goblins raided, first striking down his wife and child. No one was prepared. He fought, but his body was pierced with arrows. He died enraged…He cursed himself."

"No doubt he held a hatred for Goblins when he died," Grug added. "Where is his body?"

"The soil took him," Avaleigh sighed, holding an astonishment in her tone. "In his last breath, the ground took him. This caster knew Nature magic."

"Does the vision show you how to cast the Nature spell?!" Hayden asked excitedly.

"No," Avaleigh answered. "But he had a journal with him when the attack began. He dropped it by the fence line over there."

She pointed toward a small animal coral, which now remained untouched from the hamlet fires. Hayden and Grug followed Avaleigh to one of the fence posts where she knelt in the dust. Her hands wrapped around a small, leather-bound booklet that she knew would have to wait to be read till morning.

Avaleigh's eyes peered up to see the apparition of the journal's owner. At first, she believed it to be just part of the vision. But his eyes were staring at her, and he mouthed an unusual phrase. The girl heard no sound from the phantom figure, yet she began to mimic the apparition's lips.

"Avaleigh?" Hayden said. "Are you seeing a ghost guy mouthing something too?"

"Do you see him?!" Avaleigh asked, surprised.

"Most certainly," Hayden answered. "What is he saying?"

"I think he's uttering the words of the curse he placed on himself," she said. "I think he regrets casting it. But I've never broken a curse before."

"There's usually a deed that needs to be done to break it," Grug interjected. "Can you decipher what he's saying?"

"Do you see him too?" Hayden asked Grug.

"No," the Goblin replied. "But I've watched casters do stranger things than see what I cannot."

"Lay stones in the garden. The day shall break with light and pardon," Avaleigh uttered. "I'm sure that's what he's saying."

"Garden stones most likely refer to graves," Grug said. "If we build a memorial of gravestones for him, and likely for his family, then he shall likely be free from the curse he laid upon himself."

"I agree," Avaleigh agreed. "But we will gather as many bones as we can and bury them together."

"You think he used the bones of the slain?" Grug asked.
"Sounds creepy enough to be part of the curse," Hayden admitted.

The Goblins spread out and found the bones and the other bodies, gathering them together and placing them respectfully in the garden of the hamlet that was located next to one of the larger barns. Avaleigh noticed the garden held a chiseled sign, dedicating the garden to "Dresel, beloved wife of Caster Homgrid." Homgrid's name appeared in the journal Avaleigh picked up, exactly where it was in her vision, and it held an inscription of dedication from his wife Dresel. Thus, the pieces of the puzzle were brought together. And as sunlight stretched over the horizon, it kissed the gravestones dedicated to Homgrid, Dresel, and the child who had a marked stone with the name Selvina as written in Homgrid's journal. Several other gravestones were dedicated to the wonderful folks of the hamlet. Avaleigh watched Homgrid's apparition fade from her view and the sunrise brought more light to the world and she heard

Hayden breathe a huge sigh of relief.

"Thank goodness," Hayden said.

"Farewell, Homgrid," Avaleigh whispered. "Thank you for showing us what to do."

"Lem is not much further," Grug interrupted the girl's thoughts. "We do need to hurry and warn them."

"But first, we rest," Hayden replied incessantly. "I don't care if more monsters come along. I'll die if I don't get to sleep."

7

Bout of the Siblings

On the third day, the sun touched the middle of the clouds rolling in from the east. It was not long after the playfully white and fluffy sky turned menacingly dark. The two young casters and the Goblins reached Lem, surprisingly to Grug without further incident, just as the rain began to fall, so soft at first and soon became an unforgiving downpour to flood the entire landscape. It had become something the dwellers of Lem were used to in the spring. And why not? They welcomed every drop, as Lem is surrounded by farmlands of rice coupled with nut orchards that stretch almost to the forest in the east—a place with no name, only a reputation. Large stone walls were erected along its borders to keep monsters from coming into the farms of Lem. It also separated Lem from a hostile Goblin tribe, located within and along the mountain peaks just north of the forest.

The town itself was well put together—solid brick structures, iron gates, fortified with wooden palisades surrounding it from all sides. Several well-placed watchtowers overshadowed the land, one which saw the two young casters and Goblins approaching.

"We don't take kindly to Goblins here," one of the guards shouted from above.

"Your mother is expecting me," Grug called back.

"Is that you Grug?" The guard chuckled. "She's grown ugly as you are, so you can have her."

"Well met, Argus," Grug called back. The guard climbed down the watchtower and approached the Goblin.

Argus was a slender-built man, strapped in leather armor, with dark hair to his shoulders, a large bow in hand, and plenty of arrows in his quiver. He had a slightly noticeable scar running down his left cheek just below his left eye. He extended his forearm to Grug and the Goblin met it with his own in a tremendous clap.

"Why is your face so red?" Hayden asked his sister who turned and slapped him on the back of his neck.

"No reason," she gritted her teeth. "Just keep your mouth shut."

Hayden stood confused and rubbed where his sister struck, trying to piece together what had just happened. He could feel his eyelids were trying to stay shut, and he figured his sister was cranky from not sleeping either. For Grug had not allowed them to do so despite the young boy's adamant plea.

"We need a place to rest," Grug cut the pleasantries short.

Argus obliged and escorted them into town. The clouds above

fully opened over them as they walked the streets to an inn. Along the way, Grug began telling Argus of what they encountered—the Goblin caster in Tolin, and the destroyed hamlet just north of Lem with the Bonecrackle curse. Argus was glad to hear Grug's news but informed him that Lem already knew what befell the hamlet.

"A few escaped the onslaught," Argus explained. "They were able to make their way here—exhausted and wounded. Doubtful they will return and rebuild, especially when a Goblin tribe is warring."

"Any idea why they are pillaging outside their territory?" Grug asked.

"We do not," the guardsman admitted. "I've known you'd be back for some time, which is why I've given orders to our guards to not shoot on sight."

"You've given orders?" Grug asked. "Does that mean…?"

"Appointed me Captain of the Guard…yes, just this last winter," Argus grinned.

"Congratulations!" Came Grug's heartfelt reply. "There is no one better."

The door to the inn swung open. Hayden's eyes suddenly widened seeing a large animal skewered over a large firepit in the middle of the room. It was a Brutal Swine, slowly spinning on a rotisserie, and boiling fat dripping from the carcass. The entire inn danced with the aroma of pork.

"One of the best things about Lem is we do know how to cook Brutal Swine," Argus noticed Hayden's mouth drooling. "There's plenty here you can have, but mostly it goes to feed the guards."

"How do you stay so thin?" Hayden asked, making the captain chuckle.

"I do more running than you think," Argus answered with a bit of laughter.

While Hayden forgot about his exhaustion and did his best to eat his body weight in barbecued Brutal Swine, Avaleigh didn't eat much. Her mind remained fixated on the curse she lifted—or rather, the man she had freed from his rage. She found a quiet corner of the dining hall to remain in her contemplation. For what disturbed her was the anguish of death that drove Homgrid to cast the curse in the first place. It reminded her of what her father once told her, the time she too became enraged about losing her pet owl to a stray cat. He said, "Death will always affect life, but it never means life should end. We honor those who have lived by living, to honor what we remember of them."

Avaleigh realized the vision of Homgrid was gone from her sight, yet her mind held to the image of his face. She wanted to know more about him, to remember he was once a man, not a curse that became a monster. She opened the leather-bound journal as she had done days prior, noticing the sketches made by his hand— the intricate details of what she could only assume was his wife's face. And the babe that lay in her arms made Avaleigh long for her mother. She continued turning the pages, skimming through the sketches of streams, plants, and places, all labeled with elaborate, creative, and elegant penmanship.

"No mention of where he learned how to cast Nature spells," Avaleigh thought aloud. "He's just extremely thorough on how he feels when he's staring at trees, birds, or soil—to the poetic extreme, almost like a father."

"Sieving life through my fingers," the pages read. *"Makes the soil move. Today, I desired it would happen, and it did. With my hand stretched out, I saw it come alive and move to match my very breath. It pulsed with the very beat of my heart, and I don't know how, but I did it."*

The passage captivated Avaleigh. Homgrid mentioned in previous passages how he wished he would have been able to travel, to be chosen to study abroad, but was never given the chance. Homgrid learned Nature casting all on his own, which brought Avaleigh to concoct theories of her own. She took note that Homgrid was a caretaker of plants and animals. Spending as much time as he did with them could have sparked an understanding. At last, Avaleigh found what she was seeking toward the end of the journal, just as she had hoped. She felt she could confirm he was studying how to cast Nature Spells.

"I recall a man who came through our home, a fellow from Flemder. He claimed he heard a squirrel whispering about me, and I did not have the slightest idea what he was talking about. Then he shared with me:

Nature spells allow a caster to perform a variety of powerful spells such as understanding and communicating with animals as well as harnessing the power to push the boundaries of the earth itself.

Commune allows the caster to converse with animals. Since no spell is alike, in this way, a caster may find it easier to be friendlier with some species than others.

Landslide pushes powerful seismic waves through soil and rock but is not limited to mineral matter. It applies to metals as well. The caster can control the movement of the seismic energy, allowing it to open sinkholes, raise the soil, or simply cause destruction to the landscape. The greater mastery of this spell allows the caster to create more destructive and controlled shockwaves.

Timber Harvest gives the caster power over root systems and how they function. The more mastery of this spell, the larger the roots one can control such as making it seem like trees are alive.

Magma Infinium revolves around feeling molten rock beneath the earth and bringing it to the surface. To what end is not fairly known. It is the most powerful of all Nature spells, and is rarely achieved throughout the realms."

Avaleigh plopped her head down on her pillow, pondering all she had read, finally being able to finish reading the journal as it was difficult to do when hurrying to reach Lem for the past three days. Her mind drifted to wondering about Nature Spells and if she would ever travel to Flemder to study with other minds of casting.

The next morning, Avaleigh awoke to commotion downstairs. She could hear the sounds of insults and laughter. When she looked down from the banister of the third floor, she could see the dining hall had become packed with people, all cheering and laughing, especially at the brutal honesty of a young boy caster who lit up the ears of those around him. Grug came and stood next to her.

"That boy has a sharp tongue," he chuckled. "He already cut me from the competition."

"This is the insult competition you spoke of?" Avaleigh asked.

"It is!" Grug replied excitedly.

A slight hush came over the crowded hall. People from Lem had pressed themselves to listen through the open windows as many were unable to fit inside. An elder gentleman had just sat down in front of Hayden, his bald head and wrinkled features appeared warm and welcoming until his lips started moving. His words echoed throughout the hall.

"Every morning that I've sat, I created a better-looking scat—than the lump I see sniveling in front of me. Are you a boy? Because you look more like what I deploy—from the bottom of my gut, and to top it off, you look worse than my mangy mutt."

The crowd gasped and cringed hearing the old man insult such a young child. But then Hayden gave his reply.

"It must be true that I am a dog as I smelled your wet scat through this morning's fog. Have you no kin to help you wash between the wrinkles in your skin? You should bathe thoroughly before the boars come wisp you away to make you their bride. You're already ugly enough and your odor is killing us all with formaldehyde."

The place went in an uproar as Hayden ended his tongue-lashing. The old man, seeing he had been beaten, placed his entry on the table and got up, shaking the boy's hand with a grin to congratulate him.

"There's money in this?" Avaleigh asked Grug.

"Oh yes," the Goblin replied. "Each challenger must put in a silver coin. The winner takes the coin. The one who has the most coins by sunset is declared the winner. The rules are no one can refuse a challenge. And it seems everyone is wanting a piece of the new blood."

"New blood?" Avaleigh's face scrunched together.

"Yes," Grug explained. "Your brother has never competed. Therefore, he is considered a newcomer or new blood."

Avaleigh watched her brother put away challenger after challenger. She noticed the crowd was the decider of the winner. And the cheers for Hayden never dulled. Even when it seemed his insult was not as good in her mind, the crowd erupted during his crescendo.

The competition took a sporting break during the lunch hour and swiftly started up again sometime after. Avaleigh noticed Hayden start to dwindle a bit, coming up with insult after insult. She believed he was at risk of losing his entire pile of coins. But just as the sun was about to set, to Hayden's surprise, she planted herself down in front of him.

"This is the last one!" Shouted the innkeeper. "Let's watch the siblings tear one another apart! The challenger will go first."

Avaleigh sighed. From across the table, Hayden told her that she better not hold anything back, lest she was "chicken." Her response was anything but.

"You consume your own mass at every table, never bathing which makes your stench more potent than an unkempt stable. And for eight years I don't know why, but your pants have never been dry—constantly wetting the bed, drenching yourself from your feet all the way to your head. You whine like a piglet searching for the teat, always blabbering, to reveal your breath is just as raunchy as your feet."

Hayden's eyes widened and suddenly his ears perked up hearing the uproar of the crowd. Avaleigh saw he was doing everything he could to hold back tears. She noticed his hands clinching the table though, and she watched his lips quiver with an anger she had never witnessed. As the crowd's roar began to hush, his eyes never left his sister's face. A few moments passed and he sighed, releasing his response.

"I saw your face glow red when the captain of the guard turned his head. I'm wondering if he can break your repulsive curse with a kiss, as I hear and smell it most every night—a violent resound accompanied by a pungent mist. It's so foul that any monster it would maim. You really should give your deathly odorous spell a name. What about caster blaster, as I have witnessed more than once, it ends in an accidental disaster?"

The crowd remained silent, mouths agape. Avaleigh could feel her face had turned bright red. Her little brother now had a sinister smirk crawl across his face. Suddenly, the crowd went into an uproar. The innkeeper stepped forward raising a hand of each of the young casters.

"We have our first tie ever! What say you?" The innkeeper exclaimed, enthusiastically slapping his hands together.

The crowd resounded a thunderous approval. Each of the young casters began feeling people pat their backs and praise their wit. Avaleigh and Hayden kept their gaze upon one another. Both remained seated as the crowd dissipated and the crackling of the evening fires became the loudest noise in the hall.

"That was a little brutal," Hayden finally admitted.

"Yes, it was," Avaleigh agreed. "Maybe we should stay away from competing with one another."

"Are you kidding!" Hayden's voice cracked. "I've never heard you talk like that. I felt like I was about to cry."

"You liked that?" Avaleigh was certainly surprised.

"I had to reach super deep for that comeback," Hayden replied. "It felt like we were sparring, but with words instead of magic!"

"Well, I must say I won't be able to take it," Avaleigh said. "I don't like saying mean things about you."

Hayden got up and walked around the table. His arms reached around his sister, who embraced him back.

"I'm sorry, sis," he said. "You know half of what I said wasn't even true. You don't fart in your sleep."

"I don't?" Avaleigh's tone held a sigh of relief.

"Of course not," Hayden replied with a laugh. "You snore like a boar!"

8

Jasper

Hayden's eyes slowly opened as he emerged above the surface of the bathwater. He was exhausted but felt comforted in the saturated heat dripping down his face. The boy now held deeply to his thoughts. He had done his best to keep his sister's words from tunneling further into his mind, but her insults during the competition remained unrelenting. The boy believed he had kept a good front so his sister would not worry. But he could feel it in the moments when he gripped the table during the uproar of the crowd. His first instinct was to send a bolt of lightning straight into Avaleigh's face. It took everything he had to restrain himself, and it scared him.

Now that he had the time, he followed the advice of his uncle—"whenever anger takes hold, remove yourself from it. Step back, and learn why you are angry so that it will not make you its slave." It was sound advice. The boy knew he was not truly enraged with his sister, but still carried the weight of his schoolmates, his former best friend especially. Hayden felt scared that he had gazed upon Avaleigh as his enemy, even if for a moment.

"I don't want to see her that way ever again," Hayden told himself. "It was just a competition, and I told her to not hold back. She is still my friend."

A knock came upon his door just before he was going to slide into bed. Avaleigh stood on the other side when he opened it. She was holding Homgrid's journal, a small wooden chest, and a slight grin.

"I have our winnings," she said. "Would you like to see them?"

Hayden nodded, and Avaleigh walked inside.

"What smells like lavender?" She asked.

"Nothing," he replied swiftly, trying to mask his embarrassment from using too many pampering bath salts. "I think they lit incense or something when they cleaned the room."

Hayden appeared disinterested in the winnings, most likely due to the long day of thinking up insults to be one of the victors. Avaleigh sensed his grumpy aura but remained patient as the two sat down at the foot of Hayden's bed. The clinking of silver coins roused him to a better mood, seeing a total of one hundred tumble out upon the sheets.

"I didn't expect it would be so much!" Hayden exclaimed. His hands weaved beneath them, picking up some of the coins, and then letting them sieve through his fingers.

Also, upon the bed that Avaleigh had poured from the wooden chest was a small tattered scroll tied with a bit of twine. She picked up the scroll and held it out to her brother.

"I think you should have this," she said. "I didn't look at it, but I'm sure it has something to do with spellcasting. Maybe you can learn the spell and then teach it to me."

Hayden appeared puzzled at the generous gesture, conveying to Avaleigh that her action needed a bit more of an explanation.

"You did the heavy lifting today," she confessed. "If it wasn't for you, we wouldn't have won such a prize. And if I hadn't come along at the end, the prize would have gone solely to you."

"I don't mind sharing with you," Hayden expressed. "But thanks. It means a lot to hear you say that."

"Maybe we can buy you a new staff or something when we get to Colber," Avaleigh said. "Grug mentioned there were some fine shops in the city for casters."

"I would like that," Hayden replied but turned his gaze to the journal Avaleigh held. "Have you found out anything about Homgrid?"

"He was learning Nature spells, most likely from a pilgrim hailing from Flemder," she explained. "However, he only mentioned that the pilgrim had given him the knowledge that he could learn Nature Casting; he simply needed to follow his desire for nature."

"I don't get it," Hayden replied.

"Neither do I," Avaleigh admitted. "But, Homgrid mentioned that his love for nature drew him closer to understanding, and he had a breakthrough in learning how to cast it."

"Perhaps we should practice by hugging trees, then?" Came Hayden's lighthearted sarcasm.

"It would have been nice if he were still alive," Avaleigh ignored her brother's cheekiness, although she was glad to see his tone transform to a more positive manner. "We could have learned so much more."

Avaleigh wanted to stay with her brother to speak more on the matter. However, she could see his eyes were growing heavy. She swiftly asked who should hold onto the silver, to which Hayden was glad to give the responsibility to her should she keep her promise to buy him a "really stupendous" staff. Once she scooped up the silver from the bed, she put it into her pouch instead of the wooden box.

Upon watching his sister leave his room, Hayden couldn't help himself. He had to unwrap the scroll from their winnings. It was the only thing keeping him from plunging his face into his pillow. He untied the twine and unraveled the tiny scroll. Strangely, written on the parchment were the words:

"Hto yakjo ew eno jtupp zoyequo hto yakjo ew hto ehtok. Huro toox inhe jpaquzok unx hto yakjo jtupp kijo he onyaquzok."

The boy did his best to pronounce them. He grew tired after a while of repeating them and seeing that nothing was coming of it.

"Another riddle, just like Homgrid," he thought. His face fell against the pillow and he swiftly drifted off to sleep.

Hayden's eyes rebelled to open, but the rays of the sun peeking through his window were focused directly on them. He rolled over, hoping to sleep for another sound hour or two, yet he noticed a figure sitting in the corner of his room, staring at him, but appeared frightened.

"Hello," Hayden sat up, feeling a rush of cold swarm over him. The figure didn't answer but just kept moving its eyes around the room. The boy swiftly nabbed his staff. "I said, hello!"

"I heard you, dear boy," the figure exclaimed with a timid tone coupled with a slight lisp. "There's no need to shout. I'm simply trying to figure out where I am."

"Where you are?!" Hayden cringed. "You're in my bedroom!"

"Well, I don't remember walking through the door," the figure trembled. "It's quite frightening to suddenly see yourself sitting in the dark with a strange, loud noise from one so small."

"Loud noise?" The boy asked. "Do you mean I was snoring?"

"If that's what you call snoring, then yes," the figure replied. "I thought someone was slaying a mule."

Hayden was about to slam down a cleverer comeback, as he felt renewed to begin another round of the insult competition. However, he noticed something strange about the figure's skin as the light of the sun touched it. It was transparent. The boy eased closer to see the figure's face, recognizing him as the one and only Homgrid. But he held no aura like the vision Hayden experienced from the Tremor of Power. Instead, there were streams of icy air surrounding him.

"Are you Homgrid?" Hayden asked.

"Maybe," the apparition replied. "It could be a familiar name, something I was, but I cannot remember much."

The door to Hayden's room slowly opened with Avaleigh calling for him to get his lazy bones out of bed. She ceased to speak halfway through her wake-up call, her mouth agape at the sight of the specter sitting in the corner.

"Are you seeing this?" She gasped.

"What?" Hayden replied sarcastically. "The twitcher in the corner. Yeah, I woke up to him. Don't ask me how he got there. I rolled over, and there he was. O' and yes, before you ask any dumb questions, he definitely looks like Homgrid from the vision, but he's not sure."

"How do you not know who you are?" Avaleigh asked.

"Well, I'm not aware of who you are," the ghost bravely stood up, somewhat floating off the ground. He seemed offended by the question. "Why should I know who I am?"

"This guy is a Jasper," Hayden huffed.

Now, it would be sufficient to leave such a comment alone if one knew what Avaleigh and Hayden knew. For they branded such a man who lived in Holprice who went by such a name—a man so forgetful that he often couldn't remember to wear his trousers out in public. At times, he would see his own shadow and run straight for his house, if he could remember where he lived. Children can certainly be cruel to such an individual and often lead him into the wrong house after posing as upright citizens. Hayden had once been one of those children, and it became a game of the city folk. People would place bets on where Jasper would spend the evening, dining, and then be escorted home by responsible adults. Jasper's wife was never the wiser, as she believed he had always been at home.

"Maybe," came the specter's reply. "Jasper has a familiar ring…I think."

Hayden turned a condescending gaze toward his sister. He raised an eyebrow and began snobbishly chuckling.

"Do you even know what you are?" Avaleigh turned away from her brother.

"I feel dead," the specter admitted. "Although, I believe this is the first time I know what that feels like."

Nothing prepared the patrons for an apparition following the children down the steps of the inn. It cleared the hall of humans and

Goblins alike. All except Grug, who stared at it with a begrudging scowl. Avaleigh held up her hand to keep him from speaking, letting the large Goblin know they were not in the mood to explain yet. The only apparent thing was that the specter felt compelled to follow Hayden, and the boy kept a frown of displeasure to hear the fright prattle on about how "everything felt new and refined."

Avaleigh had a moment of clarity once they stepped outside. The sun made the specter invisible, but they could still hear him bumbling.

"Do you still have the scroll I gave you last night?" she asked Hayden.

"No, I left it on the bed," Hayden replied. "I looked at it before we left. There were words on it last night, but this morning they were gone."

"Do you remember the words?" Avaleigh hastily asked.

"No," the boy replied. "I don't."

Avaleigh surmised that the words were an incantation to release the specter. She believed he could be the very ghost of Homgrid or at least one raised from the dead that took on his appearance. One thing was for sure, the specter had certainly appeared from the result of a Conjuring cast—even if unbeknownst to Hayden.

Like the origin of most strange things, the Conjuring cast came out of Autumnwich—believed to be the workings of ancient dark Witches of the Wilds. While Conjuring spells still held a cloud of mystery for many kingdoms of the world including the inhabitants of Autumnwich, the four kingdoms had agreed on the major categories to decipher between the castings. Avaleigh, the ever-knowledgeable bookworm, began to explain to Hayden, Grug, and the rest of the Goblins what she remembered in her studies as they walked to meet Argus at his request.

Her first explanation brought their attention to the invisible Jasper, who still silently mumbled on, which began to intertwine with the soft breeze of the morn. She believed he was from the Conjuring spell known as Haunt—an unusual spell that not many who venture into Conjuring can muster, and several observations revealed dangerous mishaps, including bringing a curse to oneself.

"I feel like I'm cursed with this Jasper following me," Hayden interrupted.

Haunt reaches out into the void to bring about a spirit being that can either be a human or an animalistic apparition. Mastery of this spell is unknown, but it is theorized that increasing the strength of the apparition's power can reach the ability to bring the caster back from the dead.

Next was Replica, a spell where the caster could replicate themselves to overpower or outnumber an opponent. Growth and mastery of this spell, of course, theorized that it allowed the caster to generate more numbers of themselves with the possibility of increasing their strength or agility.

Thirdly, was Companion, a spell that allowed a caster to conjure one's, imaginary friend. Once conjured, the caster's companion grows in strength with them. However, should the companion perish, summoning them again rebirths them into a state of infancy, where they must grow and relearn what they once knew. This was the most commonly practiced spell for Autumnwich casters, and they likely imagined a solid rock Golem as their companion.

Lastly, the spell known as Minion—is similar to Companion—but casting it summoned a mindless, short creature to do the caster's bidding. However, the greater mastery of the spell allowed the caster to couple it with Replica duplicating the minion into a stronger army of dumb, yet obedient soldiers. It is also theorized that the greater the mastery of this spell allowed the caster to slightly increase the tiny stature of one's minions.

Argus was standing by the watchtower. Avaleigh felt her words begin to jumble together when he stepped forward to greet them. She let Grug move in front of her, but Hayden jumped at the first opportunity to speak up about the bodies of Goblins spread throughout the fields. There were no more than twenty, each one's face smeared in powdered white and shimmering black paint.

"They attacked us during the night," Argus said. "I'm not sure if they were testing our defenses or just desperate. Most of them appear to be starving."

"You are not wrong," Grug agreed. "If they are starving, it would stand to reason the tribe is also."

"Well, you are about to help us find out," Argus replied. "We were able to keep one alive. The Goblin is tied up in the gatehouse over there."

Avaleigh could not tell if Grug had become angry or sad. His face scrunched up when hearing Argus had captured one. For a Goblin, it is shameful to be a prisoner, especially for a warrior. Still, Grug nodded and thanked Argus for what he had done, promising he would speak with the captured Goblin. When the gatehouse door swung open, a restless creature lay breathing heavily, chained to the wall by all four limbs, like a beast. The Goblin saw Grug, the paint from its face mostly smeared off, yet it rose to its feet defiant to show any sign of weakness. Its leg still slowly dripped from the arrow that pierced it.

After a few moments, Grug began to grunt and growl—the sounds vibrating deep in his throat and huffing powerfully from his chest. The Goblin tongue was quite unusual as the two young casters noticed, this being the first time they had heard it extensively. And they remained listening for some time.

9
The Alliance

The grunts and growls in reply from the Goblin prisoner appeared stubborn and hostile. Grug took a step back and turned to Argus who awaited to hear any sort of translation.

"She says she knows I am of her kind, but my tribe has lost touch with the old ways," Grug said.

"That's a girl?" Hayden asked shockingly.

"Mind your tongue," Avaleigh snapped. "This is not the time to be sassy."

Grug laughed.

"Truly boy, your tongue was made for insults," the big Goblin continued to be amused. "If I'm honest, I have seen better features on a Scaley Dread."

This rallied Argus and the two guards with him to begin laughing as well, leaving Avaleigh rolling her eyes and the Goblin prisoner staring confused. The laughter came to a halt after a few more moments, and Argus shot back a question.

"Can she be reasoned with?" He asked Grug.

"I will remind her of the old ways," the large Goblin replied. "The Goblin tribes were once united; each tribe could invoke what we called 'gruo' which means 'help' in your tongue. The law of the tradition was that it could be invoked once every three phases of the moon. If a tribe refused to answer the call, the other tribes would raid them as punishment."

"How does that help us?" Argus inquired.

"I will invoke 'gruo' to her tribe alone," Grug said. "I will ask her to help my tribe by telling me why she is raiding Lem. If she does not comply, then I suggest we attack them and wipe them out. Otherwise, they won't stop."

"You would slaughter them?! Avaleigh's voice piped up trembling.

"It is the only way," Grug sighed. "Goblins do not cease attacking until they have what they want."

"Wait," Hayden jumped in. "You said the ones out there looked like they were starving. This one looks like nothing but bone as well."

"Do you have a point boy?" Argus asked.

"When were they not starving?" Hayden continued. "Maybe, the reason why they're attacking is because their normal food supply is gone. What's preventing them from their food source? Is there something driving them from their home? I think you should invoke your 'help' thing, but why not require she help us by allowing us to help them?"

"I'm not sure that will work," Grug huffed.

"Tell her we are casters," Avaleigh interjected. "We can help. Tell her she can allow her tribe to continue to starve or we can unite and face the problem together."

"I will try your terms first," Grug replied, finding confirmation from Argus's slight nod. "It would not hurt to see if this can end peacefully. I doubt our dear captain wants a war with a Goblin tribe on his hands."

Another round of grunts and growls, coupled now with some snarls in reply from the Goblin prisoner began. The prisoner's demeanor shifted at what the casters could only guess was a grunt that explained who they were to the prisoner. Avaleigh, however, began to have second thoughts until her brother grasped a hold of her hand.

"You're not chickening out, are you?" He whispered to her. "You've got that look."

"I don't know what you're talking about," Avaleigh whispered back harshly. "I'm simply contemplating what we should do if she agrees."

"That's easy," Hayden softly replied. "We kill the monster."

"Wait, how do you know it's a monster?"

"What else would drive an entire tribe away from its food source?"

Avaleigh smiled at her brother's wit. For a nine-year-old boy, he had an amazing tact for deducing. He had also awoken her mind from the timid thoughts running through her about the possible threat that lay ahead. Though her fears remained, she could feel her confidence ignite brighter within her soul, knowing her brother would be there with her. She turned to see Grug facing them again.

"She has conceded to the request," Grug said, his eyes appearing soft like they were about to shed tears. "I have agreed that I and the other Goblins will assist in this matter."

"What is the issue?" Argus pressed.

"It is twofold," Grug continued. "One, the tribe is being driven to raid due to a massive infestation of Spitwasps, a Goblin's natural enemy."

Spitwasps are a common pest throughout the four kingdoms— large, wasp-like insects about the size of a Goblin. They are striped gold and black down their torso, with a long stinger on their rump. They house their colony by building giant mud nests. While colonies of Spitwasps vary, it is rare

to see a nest of more than fifty to sixty at a time. Their food source is the meat of pretty much any kind, and they are mostly scavengers unless they see Goblins walking about—for some reason, Goblins are their favorite.

"Two," Grug continued with a heavy sigh. "She is part of a rebellion. The tribe is at civil war."

"Why are they at war?" Avaleigh asked.

"I will not say," Grug replied sternly. "All you must know is my axe will take care of him and the atrocities he has committed."

"I will not take no for an answer," Argus spoke up. "I will assist you in this matter. I will lead a group of archers myself to help you and the casters do what needs to be done."

Avaleigh was refreshing her memory about Spitwasps with the book she brought along with her, a diary account she kept of the different types of monsters she learned in her studies. Hayden listened to her quietly read the description, and his face became pale. She turned her gaze toward him, forgetting he hated wasps, a phobia he had never conquered.

"I can't do it," Hayden told her when they were standing outside alone. "I can't face wasps, especially not ones that size."

"We can," Avaleigh replied. "You've always helped me with my fears. Now let me help you with yours."

"You're crazy!" Hayden responded. "When have I helped you with your fears?!"

"You do more often than you realize," Avaleigh hugged him. "Besides, think of it as your chance to get revenge. You get to sting them for a change."

"O' I'm not going to stop until every one of those bugs is dead," Hayden bellowed.

"That's the spirit," Avaleigh chuckled.

It did not take long for everyone to assemble. Argus brought with him twenty archers, with quivers somewhat larger than normal. Each one also armed themselves with a sword and dagger, and each armored in leather made from Brutal Swine skin, a somewhat tougher hide to pierce. Each one had a dark green cloak and a hood covering their head. Grug and his Goblins had passed the time sharpening their weapons and strapping on their own leather armor, which appeared thicker in vital places.

"The forest is too thick for horses," Argus said. "We will travel on foot."

"I will keep an eye on this one," Grug said, holding the end of a rope to the bound female Goblin prisoner. "I have fed her some of our supplies to have the strength to stay out in front of us. She will lead us to the rebels, and from there we will devise our next move."

"I agree," Argus replied. "Let's move out."

The assemblage of humans and Goblins stood forty-strong coupled with the two young casters and one invisible specter whom Hayden suddenly spotted hovering next to him as they stepped foot in the shadows of the forest. Argus's archers almost jumped out of their armor. But the captain of the guard quickly and sternly ordered them to stand fast. The apparition was also frightened by the sudden aim of the pointy arrows in his direction.

"Calm down, Jasper," Hayden heavily sighed. "It wouldn't hurt you anyway."

"I was still startled," came Jasper's sheepish reply.

"Didn't tell us we were walking with a cursed one, captain," one of the archers spoke up, seeing Jasper speaking with Hayden.

"You are a soldier of Essend," Argus sternly replied, stepping toward the archer. "You are to be fearless, curse or no curse. However, the next time you speak insubordination to me, I will remove your tongue myself. Is that understood?"

"Yes, my lord," the archer replied with a clenched jaw.

"We don't know how it happened," Avaleigh blurted out. "But he could be useful."

"Oh really? How?" Came Hayden's sarcasm.

"Can't ghosts be invisible whenever they want?" Avaleigh asked

Jasper. "The rays of the sun do it naturally, but can't you become invisible just by wanting to?"

"I don't know," Jasper replied. "I've never tried."

"Go on then," Hayden insisted.

The specter shut his eyes. Nothing happened. He remained visible though transparent, bluish, and floating in midair.

"Not even a proper ghost," another archer whispered to the others, igniting chuckles among them.

"Wait a minute," Jasper's eyes opened, his voice filled with excitement. "I think I know what to do. Not sure why I didn't think of it before."

The specter suddenly disappeared. He grew more excited seeing the reactions of the others, knowing he had performed the task given to him.

"How did you do it?" Hayden asked.

"Well, at first, I was trying to become invisible," the ghost explained, now reappearing. "Then I thought, maybe instead of wanting to be invisible, I should try thinking about not being seen."

Jaws dropped all around.

"He's a stupid curse," an archer spoke up.

"No," Hayden corrected. "He's a Jasper."

Avaleigh explained that now they had something to scout ahead of them without being seen. Argus smiled and complimented the girl on her idea to use the specter in such a way. Avaleigh noticed though that only Hayden could give orders to Jasper. It wasn't too hard to figure out when Argus ordered Jasper to go scout ahead. "You're not the boss of me," came Jasper's snobbish reply.

"Get moving, you mindless waste of exoplasm," Hayden huffed out his annoyance.

"Well," Jasper rolled his eyes at Hayden. "You don't have to be so rude about it."

The specter turned invisible and Hayden said he could feel Jasper had left them. As they moved through the thicket of trees and brush, many of the archers quietly expressed their distrust of the specter scouting on ahead. Many of the Goblins expressed the same to Grug. However, Argus made it clear that the orders had been given to remain silent.

The collective remained moving stealthily. The forest's canopy allowed only a teensy portion of sunlight through, casting prancing shadows under the coverings of trunks and branches. To decipher a possible ambush from just another flutter of shade was impossible. Abruptly, out from the shimmering gloom, stepped a Goblin with a bow raised high in the air. Every archer spotted the creature as it rustled, but made no move to threaten them. There was a white piece of cloth tied to the top of its bow, and it slowly made its way forward. Grug bravely met the Goblin halfway, seeing it splattered with the same white and dark paint as their captive.

In small resounds of growls, grunts, and huffs, Hayden was beginning to notice the sounds were forming words to reach his ears. Avaleigh gave pause to wonder why he stared so intently. Jasper's voice whispered behind them both.

"I made my presence known to them," he explained. "I pretended to be the spirit of the forest and told them to remain peaceful toward the others. They seemed to be intrigued by the fact the two of you are casters."

"How is it you can speak Goblin?" Hayden harshly whispered back.

"I'm not sure," Jasper replied, keeping his voice low. "I simply wanted to speak their language, and then I did. And if I am thinking clearly on this, which I believe I am—as you and I are bound together—you will likely know Goblin soon as well."

"Do you understand what they're saying?" Avaleigh whispered to her brother.

"Bits and pieces," Hayden admitted. "However, the more I listen, the more those pieces are becoming fully connected."

Surprised by how intelligent her brother was sounding—even for his already high wit—his intellect seemed to expand into an unknown phase where not even Avaleigh could concoct a guess of the hows or whys. There was only Jasper, the connection between the specter and her brother. Perhaps they shared a mind, and her concern grew for Hayden. For if her brother's mind lay open to Jasper, it could mean the specter could learn everything Hayden knew, including casting. Should Jasper ever wish to become free from his bond, the specter might become quite dangerous.

The Goblin did its best to make a friendly gesture for Grug to follow, and Grug motioned for the rest of the group to tail him. Hayden made the first steps after the large Goblin, which gave more confidence to Argus and his archers who remained spread out and lingering behind until they came to a halt about a half-hour or so later.
Grug stood next to the Goblin he followed. He waved to Argus and the two young casters to join them. Once they had gathered around, two more Goblins appeared from the dense brush to meet them. Grug kept his voice hushed, yet explained their Goblin prisoner spoke the truth, and they were now standing surrounded by the rebels of the Goblin tribe. Grug untied the Goblin. She rejoined the ranks of the rebels, grunting a soft gratuitous word to the large Goblin for keeping his word. Though the others looked suspicious of Grug traveling in a large party representing another Goblin tribe, their shoulders relaxed somewhat seeing the two human casters as well as the force from Lem. One of the others stepped forward, introducing himself to Grug—the leader of the rebels, and Hayden softly relayed every word to Avaleigh.

"You bring one of our own back to us," the leader commended through a series of quiet growls and grunts. "I see you have come to war, but I do not believe it is against us. By bringing us back this one, you are not wishing to destroy us…I can assume?"

"You are correct," Grug replied. "She has spoken to us of your dire need. We are here to put an end to your raids. We know you do so because you are starving. We know you are starving because the one known as the chief of your tribe does what every Goblin knows is abominable. I have pledged to sink my axe into his head. And if not by my hand, perhaps yours. But we are here to help clear the way."

"Your words are mighty to hear," the Goblin rebel leader snorted. "Your strength is welcome with us. We do not have many arrows or weapons to fight the flying death. I will be clear, we too wish to cease our raiding, return to our home, and feed our bellies and the bellies of our offspring."

Grug relayed the conversation to Argus. The large Goblin explained the "flying death" is what humans refer to as "Spitwasp." However, there is no such word in the Goblin tongue.

The Goblin leader went on to say how young the two casters appeared. He said it was the only thing he doubted would be useful. Yet Grug dispelled his doubt by telling him of their battle against the Bonecrackles. Hayden saw how quickly the Goblin leader's demeanor changed hearing just the fine points of the tale. He replied that perhaps if they were victorious, he could ask to hear the rest of it.

The strategies began, with lines drawn in the dirt. The full force of the rebellion closed in with the new arrivals. Avaleigh counted their new numbers, estimating eighty to ninety, should lookouts still be out on their posts—most likely they were. Hayden brought his sister's attention to the location of the Spitwasp nest drawn in the soil, and the two began holding a hushed side conversation about how they would proceed to destroy it. Both sighed in disbelief when they heard the estimated numbers of the Spitwasp colony—over one hundred strong. The chief's elite guard was at least sixty or seventy strong, all taking on the build of Grug. It didn't appear to phase the large Goblin, nor his comrades. Argus pointed to several locations on the map drawn in the dust, showing where his archers would be dispersed in groups of four to help take down the Spitwasps and cover the others while they charged the village.

When evening fell, the time when the sun caresses into twilight, each one of them held their breath in anticipation—each one taking aim at their target and waiting for Argus's arrow to make the first strike. With the rest of the rebellion in place and Grug with his own clan ready to pounce, Argus let loose an arrow that screamed through the air. It landed its mark, sending a Spitwasp down to the murky waters that lay next to the tribe's village.

10

Treachery in the Marsh

The Goblin village was a series of structures made from logs and mud, elevated above the marshland. Sea waters came in from the east to rest in the spring, and by summer, the flooded land would be nothing more than muck flats and thirsty trees. However, the density of forest held well against the village's western front and tapered around to the north and south. Only the east remained exposed to a clear vision of the sea.

There, piled high from the muck in the east, the Spitwasps' nest was a mire-packed mold among the trees in the south, about a hundred or so paces from the village's southern entrance—a large wooden ramp leading up to swerving catwalks. The other entrance lay on the village's western side, but with a much narrower bridge to cross and climb up to the loft platforms. There were several of them that held rickety-looking watchtowers, and each one had a guard staring out into the distance. Just as Argus's first shot hit its mark, an uproar rang out from the one next to the south entrance.

Grug and the leader of the rebel Goblins—known as Algog—waited patiently for the Goblins in the chieftain's service to make haste to the south. The strategy was to allow for the main defense force to move toward Argus and into the arms of an ambush of rebels waiting for them in the heavy brush just in front of the captain of the guard and his archers. While the main onslaught ensued, the rebels taking the elite Goblins by surprise, Grug and Algog would lead a smaller force across the narrow bridge. Four of Argus' archers were with them, and as they began to make their move, they took out the guards in the western watchtowers. They stealthily made their way along the catwalks in search of the chieftain—it didn't take long. A flash of Thunder Strike shot through Grug's and Algog's charging lines, bringing them all to a sudden halt.

The large chief Goblin emerged from his dwelling, holding a bulky blade in one hand and a caster's staff in the other. The chief's staff held a chipped, glowing, violet rock attached to the head of the staff, much like the Goblin Avaleigh and Hayden fought in Tolin. From where she stood, Avaleigh took notice of the staff for a moment. However, she had become extremely occupied with assisting the archers against the Spitwasps. The monstrous insects had begun buzzing into a frenzy. She brought up the waters from the marsh and cast a Crashing Tide against their nest, tearing much of it down to fall into the murky waters. There were several Spitwasps in those chunks, now stunned and easy targets for arrows. Argus ordered his archers to remain focused on the ones flying toward them, taking it upon himself to finish off the ones struggling in the water. Avaleigh cast a Stormy Gale in the direction of the Spitwasps, making them fly against the chilling winds. It proved helpful for the archers as the winds held the monsters still momentarily, and they volleyed arrows into the swarm, each one hitting its mark.

Grug's and Algog's force regained their composure, noticing no one was hit, and again made their way to the chieftain, knowing his eyes were now fixed upon them. The Goblin chief cast a Thunder Strike spell again that landed heavily in the group, striking multiple Goblin rebels and one of the archers. Their lifeless bodies were jolted into the air and toppled into the waters below. Another strike did much the same, with some tensing from being electrified and crying out in agony, only to drop and be still. They had lost every one of Argus's archers just as they reached the last catwalk to stand in front of the Goblin chief. He had no guards around him. Grug desperately heaved one of his axes, but the chieftain knocked it away with his bulky sword. Yet it was worth it to buy Grug and Algog time. Algog swiftly swung mightily with a bulky sword of his own against the chieftain. The Goblin caster parried Algog's sword only to be set back on his heels to dodge Grug's swing with his other axe.

The scuffle between the three shoved the chieftain back into his quarters. It wasn't long before Grug grasped onto the axe he had thrown and began chopping away at the Goblin's bone armor plating. The Goblin caster's staff became chopped in half, which made the Goblin chieftain pull a large butcher dagger from a hidden sheath strapped to his back. Algog's swiftness and Grug's strength quickly tired the Goblin, missing to parry his opponents. Algog's bulky blade sliced through the backside of the chieftain's right knee while one of Grug's blows landed on top of the chieftain's left shoulder. Falling to his knees, the chieftain growled loudly and dropped his weapons in defeat.

"You have committed abominable acts against your tribe," Grug growled. "Your reign ends here."

"I know not what acts you speak of," the chieftain huffed. "You have just assisted the traders of the uprising, the ones who sought to use our newfound power to control the tribe."

"What are you talking about?" Grug inquired, shooting his gaze also toward Algog. "What is he talking about?"

"He lies!" Algog snarled. "He would say anything to save his life."

"The power of casters is in that stone," the chieftain motioned to the staff with the violet stone. "I have raised up mighty warriors to defend our tribe, and it has helped us make peace with the flying death. These traitors wished to control them to help them raid and pillage the humans. They sought to wage war against them and the other Goblin tribes."

"He lies!" Algog raged. "He dies now!"

Grug parried Algog's killing blow and shoved the smaller Goblin backward.

"There was another Goblin caster that I saw in Tolin," Grug grunted. "He too had a small piece of the glowing, caster stone. But he was defeated, and the stone now belongs to one of the young ones."

"Algog's brother," the chieftain answered. "If you slew him, then you rendered the betrayers powerless."

"What of this tribe?" Grug continued. "Why are you starving them?"

"They are not starving. Only Algog and the betrayers are. They were banished for their crimes. Now, I see, we should have taken their heads," the chief admitted.

Algog leaped toward the chieftain, bringing his bulky blade down once again. Grug easily parried it once more before removing Algog's head from his shoulders.

"I don't take kindly to being fooled," Grug snorted. "You will stand with me and call off your kin from my human comrades."

The chief nodded. Grug's Goblins were the only ones left to reach the chieftain's quarters. Three of them carried the chieftain toward the southern entrance, where the chieftain held up the shattered caster staff, showing his kin to cease and surrender.

The last of the swarm of Spitwasps dispersed, disappearing into the density of the trees. Argus remained confused by Grug keeping the chief alive, and he stepped out of the forest with his archers. The rest of the Goblin rebels also appeared confused, seeing no sign of Algog. The only one who wasn't confused was the female Goblin once imprisoned, now terrified. Grug could see she knew the truth was discovered. He approached her and buried his axe into her skull.

"What is this?!" Argus shouted.

"They fooled us!" Grug exclaimed to his friend. "I am truly sorry. But the rebels are the criminals, not the chieftain."

Without another word, Argus commanded his archers to fire their arrows into the remaining Goblin rebels out in the open. The rebels were too slow to react and were quickly brought down.

"Now, you will tell me what this is about," Argus demanded. He approached Grug with the two young casters holding the same look of bewilderment but with less grimace.

Grug finished explaining the situation, and Argus put up his hand to keep him from continuing any further.

"I care not for the squabbles of Goblin tribes," Argus said. "But I trust you, Grug—more than most people. If this is the course of action to keep Lem safe from Goblin raids, then I will go along with it. I do not like being fooled any more than you do. It is good we learned the truth before it was too late."

"The stone goes to the littlest caster," Grug said. "He defeated Algog's brother in Tolin, the rebel Goblin caster with a piece of the same stone."

"With that, your Thunder Strike could increase tremendously in strength," Avaleigh said to Hayden. "We'll have to get you a fancy staff to place it in."

"It is the price I have demanded they pay for our assistance," Grug said. "This way, no Goblin will be tempted to become power-hungry."

"What of the Spitwasps?" Hayden asked.

"You have destroyed their nest," Grug placed his hands on Avaleigh and Hayden. "They will likely not return. Spitwasps don't build their nest in the same place twice. The tribe should be safe, for now."

Grug then turned toward the chieftain.

"How did you control the flying death?"

"They don't like lightning," the chieftain explained. "We learned we could use them to help build up the defenses for our village, carrying bits of lumber into the marsh. Once it was built near their nest, it appeared as if we were part of their swarm."

"You controlled them through using Thunder Strike?" Grug pressed.

"Like using a whip on a slave's back," the chieftain huffed.

"My tribe no longer uses slaves," Grug replied. "We have not used slaves for generations. We are proud and strengthen our own backs to build our domain. It has strengthened us in trade and bred mighty warriors. You are a Goblin, not feeble-minded Gnolls. You could be greater should you choose to not be weak in relying on monsters to do your bidding. See what was done in a meager attack on your tribe, even though you held caster power and controlled the flying death."

"Your words ring true," the chieftain admitted. "I was a fool to believe magic would solve our problems. Perhaps your tribe can come trade with us so that we might learn from you. And from now on,

I will say your tribe is a great ally of mine, and your name will be spoken greatly in our halls."

"Our tribes would grow much stronger united," Grug said. "I will let our chieftain know of your words, and that your tribe is welcome in the north just as we will be welcome in the south."

Grug returned to Lem, his kin carrying six of their lost, while Argus returned only with twelve of the twenty archers commissioned to assist in their quest—four others being lost to the Spitwasp swarm. Grug's Goblin crew were severely battered and in much need of rest, but Hayden didn't wish to wait for them to recover. Grug understood Hayden's haste, knowing he desperately sought the trail of his father. The large Goblin could see Avaleigh felt the same.

"Warptooths may abound due to our smaller numbers," Grug explained. "But we can move out in the morning."

"You're coming with us?" Avaleigh asked.

"I am," the large Goblin responded. "I will bring only two of my kin with me. The others will wait here to recover and then return to my home with our dead to give them a proper farewell. I must also relay the message to our chieftain about the new alliance with this tribe in the south."

"I'm sure we would be fine without your assistance," Hayden's tone dripped with a saturation of excessive confidence.

"I don't doubt it," Grug returned the comment more sternly than Hayden had anticipated. "I am not doing this for you. I will prove myself trustworthy."

The two young casters stared in confusion at one another but shrugged off Grug's strange response. He changed the subject.

"I did not tell nor did I show this, not even to Argus," Grug pulled a rolled-up parchment from his cloak. It appeared like a page torn from a book or journal. "The chieftain had this on him as well. From what I can tell, it seems to be something specifically for casters."

Avaleigh took the page from Grug and unrolled it. The language was certainly foreign to her, but she thanked him as if she understood the elegant calligraphy written on the page.

11

The Meadowlands

Hayden could scarcely open his eyes, but he did his best. With a large yawn and a heavy sigh, the young caster pulled the bed covers from his sore body. Yesterday's precision casting against the swarm using his Thunder Strike had left his muscles tight. He had never had to keep such control before. But he was able to dress in a matter of minutes, splashing cold water on his face from the washing bowl as he opened the door to leave. Avaleigh again, stood on the other side with an infectious smile despite the obvious aches she had as well.

"What?" Hayden asked. "Why are you smiling like that?"

"I have something for you," Avaleigh replied. "You don't have to take it if you don't want it. However, I thought you should decide."

She pulled out from behind her back a magnificently polished dark oak caster staff with a space to inlay items. It must have been made for one with less stature than most, as its length only reached just above Hayden's head. The staff appeared nothing like that of a child's beginner staff. Glyph markings were carved up and down its swirling spine, with whittled wings and vines for its head. Hayden's face lit up.

"Where did you get this?!" Hayden asked.

"Argus had it in the armory," Avaleigh explained. "Last night, I asked him if there were any weapons in his possession not being used and wouldn't be missed. He was happy to help, and he didn't let me pay. Said it was the least he could do."

Avaleigh reached next to the door and pulled another caster staff into view. It held a lighter polished tone of ash wood and stood over a head's length taller than the girl. It also had a place to inlay items such as the caster stones in Hayden's possession. The staff's spine slightly waved back and forth from its tail to the head, where its top bent into the shape of a hand shrouded in wings.

"Unless of course, you like this one better?" Avaleigh offered. "I thought you would like the darker oak best. But you are welcome to trade."

"I like both," Hayden admitted. "You know me though. I do like the darker one. Plus, yours seems a bit too tall for me. Mine could become a walking cane as I grow taller, so I'll still look good!"

Avaleigh chuckled along with her brother as he closed the door behind him.

"And these were just in the armory?" Hayden scratched his head.

"Yes," Avaleigh answered. "He said I could keep them. He also gave me a couple of short blades, one for you, and one for me."

"No way!" Hayden exclaimed a little louder than the people still sleeping would have liked. "Father never let me handle one of these."

"These are just in case," Avaleigh warned. "We do not draw them unless we can't find the strength to cast. They're our last resort."

"Or to cut a monster's throat open to give it an epic death," Hayden laughed.

"This is not a jest," Avaleigh said stringently. "We do not use these unless we have to—understood?"

Hayden rolled his eyes and then strapped his short sword to his belt. He pushed passed Avaleigh into a strut that embellished his arrogance. She silently huffed her disapproval, but soon followed behind him. Grug was at the bottom of the stairs in the dining hall, a satchel of bread and fruit in each hand. Grug's two Goblin kin met them outside—a pair of stout yet short twins, Morlo and Porlo. Both had a jutted under-bite peeking out of their helms that encased the tops of their head, with nothing but their yellow-tinted eyes showing through. Their bodies were stout, much shorter than Grug's, but the bulk of their frames were much more athletically toned—no belly fat to point out, just hardened muscle. Had they been hurled by a trebuchet into a stone wall, no doubt they would break it down and perhaps survive the ordeal.

Hayden recalled being in proximity with them once before, in defeating the Bonecrackle caster, whose spirit now haunted him wherever he roamed. The twins had landed next to him when

Homgrid, now Jasper, cast a Sinister Cyclone spell that threw the entire party in all directions. The young boy was delighted to hear they were the ones Grug had chosen to accompany them.

"You might be right about the swords," Hayden whispered to his sister. "With these two, I doubt we'll get a chance to swing them at anything."

He, of course, didn't say such things with any sort of disappointment ringing in his tone. Instead, Avaleigh watched his eyes light up like a ruffian up to no good. It was strange to her to see the shift in her brother, swiftly becoming more and more confident while she remained unsure of herself. The joy he displayed for growing stronger was becoming wild without restraint. Yet Avaleigh saw the danger looming to possibly the day when his confidence would shatter due to defeat from another who was stronger. For it was how Avaleigh took on any opposition, thinking through all the possible outcomes and taking it on as if she were the weaker.

Once more she thought back to the betrayal of Hayden's best friend, and how cruel the other caster kids were to him. They mistreated her as well, but not so in the same capacity. Hayden was not as independent as her. While she didn't care to be alone all the time, Avaleigh did like keeping to herself while others were around. Her brother, however, needed true friendship, to feel needed by them, and to shine among them. One day, all of that was gone in a single moment. Clearly, he was still trying to break free from the fear of needing anyone ever again—perhaps, even his own sister.

Avaleigh's mind drifted to recalling Hayden limp through their father's study door after the incident. His eyes were blackened from fists slamming into his face. His nose dripped with blood. There were bruises up and down his spine and along his ribs. His ankle was sprained. He had tiny lacerations across his forehead. He had several broken knuckles, likely from his hands being stomped on. His clothes were tattered and torn. Overall, Hayden was thumped good by a boy, who was once his friend, and the other boys who he recruited to do the deed.

During his recovery, Hayden became serious about reading all he could about the spells he sought to master. The ancient blood that ran through his veins overcame most of the obstacles of understanding how to cast the spells, and he found his forte easy to cultivate. The day came when he surprised his attackers, who received minimal reprimands, as it was Hayden's word against ten others. Although the siblings' uncle knew Hayden didn't just magically acquire his wounds, yet held no proof against the ones who gave Hayden his beatdown. But Hayden knew.

One day, he confronted them in the courtyard of the monastery. Avaleigh saw her brother say nothing, but cast Thunder Strike with such intensity on the group of boys—had Hayden been any stronger, each boy would have lost their life. Only his once friend remained conscious, almost seemingly as if Hayden had planned it that way—standing over the boy like he would roast the flesh from his bones. The only saving grace of the boy not becoming a cinder and Hayden not becoming a murderer was their uncle's magisterial bellow that stayed in Hayden's hand. From then on, Hayden was taught separately from the other children. Avaleigh joined him due to her uncle noticing the immense growing fear of their bloodline. It caused fear toward Avaleigh, not just from the children, but from parents as well.

Stepping out in the direction of Shroe, they bid Argus farewell, and Lem grew smaller behind them as they stepped jauntily along. Hayden began an insult challenge almost immediately with Grug who gladly joined in, with Morlo and Porlo grunting their pleasure in hearing the banter. Avaleigh remained deep in her thoughts, though enjoying seeing her brother smile more than she had seen him of late.

Now, the road from Lem to Shroe zigs more than zags and twists into the meadowy hills as one travels between the two mountain ranges. It is a meadowed valley of wildflowers, tall grass, and scattered skinny trees. And as Grug suspected, it was no surprise that a smaller party would attract the hungry mouths of four-legged canines with protruding, jagged teeth. A stiff breeze brought their scent to his nostrils before the howling began. Warptooths can be smelly creatures should they not be domesticated and remain unbathed.

"Finally!" Hayden sighed as Grug relayed the warning. "Let's fry up some dog."

"Stay on the road," Grug said. "Keep away from the long grass."

Hayden felt Avaleigh's back press against his. He grinned again.

"Are you ready to test out our new staffs?" He asked.

"I do like the way it feels," Avaleigh admitted. "Of course, I believe there might also be a Tremor of Power nearby."

"Then it should go to you," Hayden said. "Cause I don't feel anything, yet."

The Warptooths were not aggressive in their approach, but remained cautious, circling the five, and keeping a safe distance in the long grass.

"Why don't you go take a look, Jasper?" Hayden said aloud. "How many Warptooths are there?"

"I believe I can see them just fine from here," the specter replied. "No need to put me in harm's way."

"What can harm a ghost?" Hayden exclaimed; his eyes pulsed with perplexity. "Get out there and tell us how many there are!"

"You certainly seem to constantly hurt my feelings by barking orders at me," Jasper rang out a feeble, yet rebellious reply. "Warptooths are frightening creatures."

"They can't hurt you!" Hayden shouted.

"That doesn't mean I'm not frightened," Jasper whimpered.

"Of all the things to be cursed with, I'm cursed to be haunted by a cowardly specter," Hayden huffed. "Look, just fly above them where they can't reach you. Count how many there are and let us know."

"You may have a point," Jasper admitted. "But it wouldn't hurt to ask a little nicer next time."

"You could be a little nicer," came Grug's grunt to Hayden.

"Yes, Hayden," Avaleigh added. "The poor thing is dead, but he does have feelings."

"I can't believe I'm hearing this," Hayden said aloud, feeling the specter fly upward.

"He seems depressed," Avaleigh continued. "I mean, how would you feel if you were dead all the time and had to follow someone around who barked orders at you? I don't think you'd like it very much."

"Fine…" Hayden sighed in frustration. "I will try to be nicer. Although, if I were dead all the time, I wouldn't have to worry about how many Warptooths want to eat me."

The howling ceased from the pack as Jasper came to Hayden with the news of counting only six Warptooths surrounding them in the long grass. Suddenly, the canine monsters became still and quiet now. Grug slightly voiced his confusion with their behavior. He suggested they continue cautiously onward along the path. Avaleigh tilted her head, befuddled, as she pointed toward a large figure flying through the skies. Its shape was nothing more than a silhouette. But by seeing its large-scale size and long, outstretched feathered wings, she identified the monstrosity.

Grug was no stranger to the creature's behavior as he told the others to move quickly along the path, keeping low as they went. He pointed to a clump of trees a couple of hundred strides up the ridge. For if the flying monster was on the hunt, it would likely guard its prey the way it guarded its nest.

"I have not known one to venture so far away from the mountains," Grug admitted. "From its size, I would say it is a male."

The black streaks along the creature's feathers came into view. Its black talons were agape, with its beak screeching a deafening cry toward its prey. It swooped between Avaleigh and her brother, Hayden, falling behind. The rush of wind slammed against the boy's chest, knocking him onto his back while the girl got shoved to her knees. She caught herself before her face planted into the ground and turned to see her brother trying to catch his breath. Grug and the other Goblins had quickly turned back and already nabbed Avaleigh to her feet. Hayden could see the monster had pounced on a Brutal Swine that lay hidden in the tall grass, no more than a dozen paces away.

"So that's a Blighttalon," he thought dazed and aloud, as he felt Porlo's strong hands lift him to his feet.

The creature was still flying about when the five of them reached the trees. It became apparent that the Blighttalon believed the Warptooths were a threat to its kill, and it proceeded to respond aggressively toward them until they dispersed. The Blighttalon began tottering along the ground toward the Brutal Swine carcass, its wings tucked delicately at its sides.

"I see the Tremor of Power, now," Hayden told his sister. "It's coming from that thing."

Avaleigh turned to see her brother was not mistaken. An emission of power emanated from the giant feathered fiend that almost felt like a voice calling to her mind.

"I think it's best we leave this one where it is," she said.

"I agree," Hayden sighed heavily. He pulled open his shirt to see a large bruise forming on his chest where the air slammed into him as the Blighttalon swooped by.

"We best keep moving," Grug said. "We don't want it to mistake us for threats too."

A day into the journey, the others could see Hayden falling behind. Grug thought it likely he had a couple of bruised ribs that needed time to heal. But it made the trek grow to a crawl until the twin Goblins had the bright idea of taking turns carrying the boy on their shoulders with the boy's chest gently resting against the back of their bulky Goblin heads. Even Grug started taking a turn when the twins challenged him to see who could carry the boy the longest.

Now somewhat higher in stature, Hayden took the opportunity to be the lookout, keeping a sharp eye on the skies. Should he have watched the meadow fields more closely, he may have noticed the silent slithering serpents stalking them on till dusk.

There are many monsters in the world—none of which are as fanciful in remaining intrinsically camouflaged and patient for the right moment to strike the unaware prey. Avaleigh would have known the dangers of such a monster being so close by had she seen them. But it is not always apparent as to where a pair of Glowserpents shall roam, as most prefer solitude throughout the four kingdoms.

Glowserpents grow to become large, carnivorous snakes that have the ability to blend their skin to their environment and can cast Thunder Strike, glowing bright gold just before they are about to do so. A Glowserpent's Thunder Strikes is not deadly, though it does paralyze what is stricken—just enough time to

GLOWSERPENT

be wrapped in the serpent's coils, slowly crushed to death and devoured whole. Glowserpents are masters of stealth despite their massive size which can range from ten to fifty feet long depending on their age. Unusually compared to most other monsters in the wilds, a Glowserpent's greatest survival skill comes with another spellcasting ability—a manifestation of Allay that heals the monster over time. While they hunt practically anything that draws their attention, they are not commonly fond of getting too close to large populations of humanoid creatures, or fire, and tend to avoid the scent of lavender.

Unfortunately for most serpents of the world, including Glowserpents, Goblins have a nose that can pick up their scent should they venture too close or hide downwind, where the night air carried the serpents' odor to a large Goblin who suddenly felt his instincts perk up.

Grug didn't speak of them as the campfire roared to life, and Hayden laid his head down, unaware of the danger. But Avaleigh noticed how the others were staring ominously at one another. She didn't raise the alarm, wanting Hayden to rest without worry. Grug sensed her unease.

"The three of us will take turns keeping the fire going," Grug said, seeing that Morlo and Porlo had found plenty of firewood well away from where the serpents hid. "Most monsters don't like fire much anyway. You two young casters can sleep soundly. No telling whether we'll be facing a Blighttalon tomorrow."

12

Predators' Road

Avaleigh flopped down next to Grug, who was keeping his nose to the night air. The other Goblins were lying close to Hayden, and gripping their weapons tightly during their slumber as the girl noticed. She inquired about the Goblin's strange behavior and waited patiently for him to reply.

"We're certainly being hunted," Grug whispered after a few moments had passed. "The Glowserpents have kept pace with us."

"What are Glowserpents doing in the Meadowlands?" Avaleigh asked.

"It is unusual," Grug admitted. "I've never run into a Glowserpent in the meadow pasture. But what's more unusual is that there are a pair of them hiding out in the tall grass behind us, no more than, perhaps, a couple of deer bounds away."

Avaleigh was not familiar with this estimated unit of measurement. Grug saw her puzzled mug and explained it was a Goblin phrase for what humans commonly referred to as "too close for comfort."

"You can smell them?" Avaleigh asked. "How is that possible?"

"Goblins can smell a lot of things," Grug replied. "Scent is how we naturally commit things to memory. For instance, I can still smell the lavender flowers you took with you from your room back in Lem. Glowserpents are not fond of its odor. Although, it won't keep them at bay if they sense something is wounded—as that is easy prey."

"Do you suppose they're hunting my brother because he appears injured?"

"I wouldn't doubt it," Grug sighed, then took another whiff from the gentle breeze. "I picked up their scent a little while after we encountered the Blighttalon. I didn't carry Hayden until I was sure the Glowserpents were staying at a safe distance."

"It would seem they are looking for a window to ambush us," Avaleigh felt her heart thumping a little harder.

Grug nodded.

"Then we must rid this threat from the road. We must not only protect my brother but anyone else who travels this way. Warptooths and a Blighttalon are enough to worry about."

The girl clenched her staff. Grug stared at her, surprised by her burst of bravery. Or perhaps it was simply...

One distraction was all it took. Avaleigh leaped to her feet seeing a flash of golden hue. A Thunder Strike bolt slapped against Grug's back which sent him flying over the campfire. He remained in paralysis. His outcry, however, woke the twins. They were up on their feet in no time, seeing the enormous serpents enter the light of the fire and begin encircling them. Porlo grabbed a stick from the fire and hurled it in the direction of the serpent, making it retreat from the torch.

Avaleigh could see the eyes of the serpents. Their eyes were a glistening black, swirling with a green mist. Both were at least twenty feet long by her estimate, and both of their skins were beginning to glow gold. The girl had already swarmed herself with water vapors accumulated from the air. She waited to time her strike, seeing the serpent heads' draw closer together. Avaleigh brought forth a wave of water that slammed against them as they opened their mouths to elicit their Thunder Strike. Her time could not have been more perfect. The bolts erupted inside their mouths, and each reared back to regain their composure.

The open window for Morlo and Porlo allowed them to let loose arrows toward the serpents, both hitting their mark. The arrows landed in the eyes of one of the serpents, and the monster rolled back into the long grass. The other Glowserpent brought its head in to strike Porlo, who barely avoided the serpent's fangs. Morlo slammed one of his axes into the skull of the serpent, but it did nothing more than make the monster rear back to reassess its next strike. Porlo immediately shot another arrow off, landing just under the serpent's underjaw. The arrow pierced its mark, which let Avaleigh know where the Glowserpent was vulnerable.

"Go for its underbelly," she called to the twins as she summoned an icy gale of wind.

The girl's Stormy Gale did not slow the monster as she had hoped. Instead, the serpent's eyes turned toward her, and its body blocked any projectiles from piercing its eyes. The serpent opened its mouth getting ready to strike. Avaleigh could see the arrowhead that had pierced through the bottom of its jaw, which inspired an idea, but one she never risked before. She focused the casting of her Stormy Gale around her making every bit of water vapor turn to solid ice and bringing the pieces together in one large, floating, ice shield.

The Glowserpent was already in mid-strike when the shield solidified. With half of the serpent's body airborne, the serpent's head crashed into the ice, only knocking itself senseless. As it fell to the ground, Avaleigh focused her Crashing Tide, casting it to lift the water from the ground which suddenly turned to spikes of ice, a cold bed of puncturing fatal pricks for the serpent's underbelly. When it landed, one of the spikes protruded straight through its jaw and into its skull. The girl exhaled letting the enormous shield fall and shatter against the ground. She saw, out of the corner of her eye, an axe swing down against the serpent. It was Grug.

Again, he swung his axe, chopping through the serpent's hardened top exterior, chopping until its head was completely off.

"Find where the other one went," he grunted at the others. "It can't heal without its head."

"What do you mean heal?" Avaleigh asked, fully bewildered. "The thing is dead."

"Glowserpents are never dead until you hold their separated skull in your hand," Grug replied. "Their allay magic works even in death. That's why Goblins call them 'Naga Necroman,' or serpent sorcerer in your tongue. Removing the head is the only way to make sure they stay dead."

Morlo and Porlo did not take long to return with the head of the other serpent. They had found it unconscious just off the road in the long grass. The two Goblins were boasting about their incredible archery skills when they realized they had awoken Hayden. The poor boy had passed out and slept through the entire encounter.

"What is that?!" The boy cried, his eyes popping wide.

"It's a Glowserpent," Avaleigh replied. "How were you able to doze through all the noise?"

"I don't know," Hayden shrugged.

"We need to leave," Grug interjected. "We don't want to wait for more predators to find us."

The howling of Warptooths had already begun to echo in the distance and continued drawing closer as the sun peeked above the horizon. Avaleigh turned to see the monstrous canines bearing down on them in the dim light of the morn. This time, the Warptooths were charging in with more numbers than she was able to count.

"How many are there Jasper?" Hayden shouted, seeing the fiends were encircling them.

"I count seventeen," the specter replied.

"Everyone duck!" Hayden shouted again.

The boy was not going to wait for the Warptooths to make the first move. He sent forth a plethora of short bursting Thunder Strikes, casting them wildly in all directions—tailing another type of Thunder Strike accompanying his previous casting that manifested a long bolt of lightning into one stream connected to his staff. He swung it around like a whip, snapping it against several Warptooths who either fell dead or stunned depending on how long the bolt sparked against their flesh.

While the others remained low so as not to be hit, Avaleigh began to bring together water vapors to create a wave that swiftly manifested to encircle the group. She continued to speed up the wave that began to move like a whirlpool. Warptooths charging in that somehow escaped Hayden's lightning whip were swept up into the vortex, spitting the beasts out in the center, half-drowned or fully—it did not matter to the Goblins as they slammed their axes into each one's skull.

"Can you hold this spell, Avaleigh?" Hayden cried out over the noise of howling and rushing water. He had ceased casting, showing he had fatigue and cringed from the pain of his bruised torso.

"I can," she called back. "Let's make it a little wider so we have more room."

The swirling wave expanded, and Hayden asked Jasper once more to count the Warptooths.

"I see twelve," Jasper replied. "Barely a dent if you ask me."

"I wasn't," Hayden grunted his retort.

Morlo and Porlo started aiming their arrows at the Warptooths, but Grug commanded them to not fire. The wave suddenly sped faster, swirling high above them, but they could see through the water clearly to notice a different species of canine monster had begun to assert its dominance over the pack of Warptooths, killing four swiftly to make the others scamper away.

"How long can you keep this wave going?" Grug asked.

"I'm not sure," Avaleigh admitted. "I don't feel tired yet, but I do feel warmed up. Why?"

"Because there's a pack of Ash Hounds that just came in," the Goblin replied.

Ash Hounds are the only canines known to breathe fire. They have dark gray fur with streaks of violet

ASH HOUND

and are extremely aggressive, traveling in packs of no more than six. While they may appear frail due to their unusually thin appearance, their strength is not to be underestimated as they only harbor an estimated one percent of body fat, and their skin is almost as dense as bone.

Avaleigh saw a flash burst from one of their mouths, a ball of flame that quickly dispersed against the rushing water. The others joined in, hitting the wave again and again with fire.

"They're testing it," Grug explained.

"How rested are you?" Avaleigh asked Hayden.

"I think I can start up again," he grinned as he placed his feet beneath himself to stand. The boy gingerly stretched for a moment and then gripped his staff tightly with both hands. "I'm going to send them flying."

The manifestation of the Sinister Cyclone came as a surprise to the hounds. Avaleigh shoved the wave outward, knocking the four hounds to the ground while Hayden's Sinister Cyclone swirled around to pick up all four of them. The monsters tumbled around, yelping as they ascended higher into the sky. When Hayden thought it was high enough to dissipate the spell, he let them drop to their doom. What wasn't accounted for was the fifth—a clever Ash Hound that remained patient in the long grass. The boy never saw the vicious jaws clamp down on the back of his neck as the fifth Ash Hound pounced on him.

Avaleigh's rage was instant, a sister afeared to seeing her brother's demise and refusing to allow the beast responsible to remain to live. She conjured another wave of water that swooped in to encapsulate the hound, pulling it away from her brother's limp body. She manifested Stormy Gale, chilling and hardening the ball of water, trapping the Ash Hound in a solidified, icy tomb.

Grug and the other Goblins could not believe what transpired, seeing how pale Hayden's body suddenly became, and the splatters of crimson strewn around him. Avaleigh had no words but gasped continuously with tears streaming violently from her eyes. She gripped Hayden's body so tight that not even Grug could separate her from it.

"We will take him to Colber with us," Grug reassured. "I'm so sorry little one."

Avaleigh peered upward to see Grug's face holding sympathy for her loss. Although, she spied something peculiar hovering just above them. It was Jasper staring down at Hayden's lifeless body.

"Are you not free now?" She asked the specter, who did not turn away from Hayden's face. "My brother is gone. Your curse is finished."

Without a word, Jasper kept his concentration and reached through the skin of Hayden's chest. A loud crack came from Hayden's neck as if something had been put back into place. Another moment came when Avaleigh felt her brother's lungs inhale. Abruptly, his eyes popped open, fervently gasping for breath. The boy grabbed his chest, agonizing from Jasper pumping his heart to beat once more. The specter released his hold and Hayden began to reach a calm.

"From now on, he will see through my eyes," Jasper confessed. He turned his face to Avaleigh. "Remember, I'm not the one who's cursed, but it is your brother. The Sight of the Dead has now awoken within him."

13
The Primitive Riders

Hayden remained startled as his sister and Grug helped him to his feet. He reached up to feel the back of his neck, knowing it had been maimed and broken by a wild beast. Yet his mind could not comprehend where he had gone or where he had come from. He began screaming, his eyes growing bloodshot as if possessed by some madness.

"What's wrong with him?" Avaleigh demanded of Jasper, who was now disappearing as the sun's light crept into the day. "What do you mean he has the 'Sight of the Dead.'

"I know not how I know," the specter replied. "Perhaps it is the will of the curse. Your brother cannot die. He now sees what I see—a dim hue of sapphire clouding the warmth of the day. His mind cannot comprehend it, but he shall see other things, I'm sure. Should he be slain again, his sight shall grow ever darker until he becomes a nightmare himself."

Hayden suddenly ceased his screaming, standing and remaining in a state of dismay. Yet he breathed slowly, staring toward the horizon, and not responding to his sister trying to speak to him.

"How did this happen?" Grug asked Avaleigh.

"There was a scroll in our winnings," she answered. "He must have read the incantation correctly."

"Sounds like something created by a Witch of Wilds," Grug admitted. "Not many of them left, but they were always creating their own type of magic. Sorry, love."

"Maybe the casters in Colber can help us," Avaleigh wiped tears from her eyes. "Maybe they can set him free, and Jasper's spirit can be freed as well."

"Perhaps," Grug shrugged. "But we best move on. Even I'm afeared to face another night on this road."

Warptooths gathered once more but followed at a distance behind them as they continued onward. Their howling kept each one of them on edge with the exception of Hayden, who was being carried by Grug. The boy's composure kept improving. However, as Shroe came into sight, none of them could believe their eyes. In the distance, they could see the decimated town as clouds of smoke spewed into the skies. Even the caster shrine, a once large and steepled architecture lay smashed to pieces and abandoned. Grug quickly led the others off the road to hide.

"What do you suppose happened?" Avaleigh whispered.

"There was a slaughter," Hayden mumbled, his glazed eyes staring out toward Shroe. "I can see the dead. I can still sense their terror."

"Are you seeing visions?" His sister asked.

"The dead here still speak," he replied. "They are still crying out. I see beasts, a Feliformia but stand upright like a human, a snout like a canine, strength like a bear, spotted fur, and move swiftly like felines in the wild."

"Sounds like Gnolls to me," Grug kept his distaste to a low growl. "But Gnolls are notorious for being extremely unintelligent, prone to infighting, and love to let others do hard work for them. The only way they would attack a place like Shroe is if they have somehow become united…again—or one of them holds some sort of intelligence to unite the tribes."

"Or power," Avaleigh interjected. "We've seen Goblins use caster stones before. Is it likely these Gnolls have found one as well?"

"Could be," Grug surmised. "Though, I can see our path cannot go through Shroe. We must head north and proceed to Colber's eastern gates."

"No," Avaleigh said firmly. "We cannot waste any more time. We don't even know if the Gnolls headed north. We should stay hidden until nightfall, then proceed on course to Colber."

"Gnolls will see us just as clearly at night as during the day," the large Goblin explained. "What we would need is something to outrun them."

"They look like mounted troops to me," Hayden said, pointing toward a large ban that had appeared in Shroe.

"Those are the Primitive Riders from Colber!" Avaleigh's face lit up. Her excitement was no surprise to the Goblins. Seeing the Primitive Riders of Colber for the first time leaves a sense of wonderment— plate armored soldiers holding a long lance in one hand and a large oval shield in the other, with a curved blade strapped to their back. Each one wears a bright sapphire paludamentum, with the emblem of Essend's golden stag. The reason for their name came from their specialty recognizable mount. Other mounted troops in Essend ride on horseback, while these riders of Colber are harnessed to the backs of Primitive Banes.

Primitive Banes are bulky primate creatures standing at least twice the height of any normal human, with black fur, sharp fangs, and a grip that can easily crush bones or rip apart most things, even iron bars. Wild Primitive Banes mainly inhabit Essend's largest forests, Ogrin and Gombder. Colber is known for domesticating them as

PRIMITIVE BANE

steeds, using them for hauling trade goods within the Trade Triangle that includes Colber, Arwal, and Prave. Some are bought and sold— pricey to purchase but are illegal to sell to anyone not of Essend.

Primitive Bane mounts are strapped with their own special armor—hardened leather guarding their hind legs, chests, and shoulders. Each one is controlled by a rider's knees, leaning, and pressing significantly against either the right side or left side of the trapezius.

Being in Holprice her whole life had never allowed Avaleigh to see the spectacle she read about. Her memory held only sketches from historical documents, but now seized a living embrace of such a sight.

"We must get to them before they leave," she insisted to Grug, who was not appearing thrilled to rush out so hastily.

Hayden already slipped passed them and had walked confidently into the clearing. Avaleigh looked up and many more Primitive Riders appeared behind the very few. Seeing their haste toward Hayden was intimidating, even frightening. She ran to him, leaving the Goblins where they were hiding.

The Primitive Riders soon surrounded Hayden and herself, close to thirty in all. She could hear the knuckles of the beast mounts thump the ground as they encircled them. Soon they remained still and one of the riders spoke.

"Ones so small…" the rider huffed, removing her helmet. "I feared we would not find any others. How long have you been in hiding?"

"Not long," Hayden said sarcastically.

"Forgive my brother's impertinence. He has not been himself," Avaleigh interjected. "We are not survivors of whatever has befallen here. We are on our way to Colber accompanied by three of our companions, the Goblin tribe north of Holprice."

"You have traveled from Holprice, then?" The rider asked.

"We have," the girl said politely.

"Your Goblin friends can come out," the rider assured. "We have no quarrel with Goblins. What you see of Shroe is the doings of Gnolls."

Grug heard the rider's words, faintly from where they hid. He slowly stepped out with Morlo and Porlo following behind him. The rider's circle opened to allow them to pass to the leading rider, who revealed a grin showing she knew the large Goblin.

"I should have known you would pop up again, Grug," the rider said. "Last we met, we were in Prave, yes?"

"You are correct, Lady Sheen," Grug bowed.

The Lead Rider's dark hair drooped elegantly over one eye. She pulled it back revealing a slash scar above it, one that traveled up to her hairline. Her brown skin glistened with sweat that she properly dabbed from her brow.

"What brings you westward, then Grug?" She asked, almost with a demanding tone. Her emerald eyes remained attentive to Morlo

132

and Porlo, trying to recall if she had seen them before.

"We are traveling to Colber," Grug confessed. "These two young casters are seeking counsel from the Elder Caster there."

"What business do you have with the Elder Caster?" Lady Sheen inquired.

"Begging your pardon, Lady Sheen," Avaleigh stepped in. "We are not at liberty to say. We need the Elder Caster's counsel on a private matter. Grug, Morlo, and Porlo vowed to escort us to Colber after assisting Lem with a small problem with a Goblin tribe. My brother and I met Grug and his Goblins on the road to Tolin when we left Holprice."

"You are casters from Holprice?" Lady Sheen said incisively. "Are you on a pilgrimage, then?"

"Something like that," Hayden said smugly. "We believe it to be something more important than that."

"Once more, forgive my brother," Avaleigh intervened. "He is not himself."

"The lot of you appear worn out," Lady Sheen observed. "You shall ride with us back to Colber. My dear, you shall ride with me."

Avaleigh could hardly contain her excitement as she stepped up into the Primitive Bane harness. Lady Sheen did her best to pry more information from the young caster, as Avaleigh knew she would. But the young girl remained polite and divulged nothing further about their purpose of traveling to Colber. She even offered to speak with Lady Sheen after they sought the Elder Caster's guidance on the matter, alluding to the Lead Rider that she could perhaps be of help later.

As they rode through the remains of Shroe, there were still fires burning bright. It was difficult to comprehend the once well-fortified town's several stone walls surrounding it had become toppled, with the bodies of soldiers strewn along the ruins. Undoubtedly, they had fought desperately to defend it. The carnage became trapped in the young casters' minds, and even Grug had never seen the likes of what Gnolls can do, especially when they are unified and not fighting amongst themselves.

"Shroe was a holy place," Lady Sheen spoke to Avaleigh moments after they left the inflamed town behind. "I have gone there many times during my leave to find rest from the things I've seen. The casters there knew much in the ways of Allay, and, likely, many of the records of their discoveries are now lost."

"Were there survivors?" Avaleigh asked. "Are there any casters who escaped that still hold knowledge of Allay casting?"

"Some," Lady Sheen replied. "But not many. Most of the survivors we saw running toward the gates of Colber were simply citizens of the city."

"How long ago was that?" Avaleigh asked.

"About four days," Lady Sheen said. "It is strange to see the fires are still burning. It's as if the stones are fated to be ablaze in the flames of war day and night. I suspect the Gnolls continue to return and set fire to the rubble after we've departed."

"Grug suspects the Gnoll tribes have united," Avaleigh continued the conversation. "Do you suspect the same?"

"I do," Lady Sheen replied. "The Gnoll tribes almost always war amongst themselves apart from a few times in our history. If my memory serves me correctly about the past of Essend, the Gnoll tribes have only united twice—once during the establishment of Colber's fortress, which forced them to find new lands. The other was approximately two generations ago when a Witch of Wilds found a way to commune with them, convincing the tribes to act as one against Colber and Dundlen."

"Do you suppose Dundlen is also in danger?"

"It is likely," Lady Sheen continued. "Messengers were sent with escorts to warn them. But we have not heard anything come back."

The band of Primitive Riders held close to two hundred, setting out to Shroe after survivors stumbled into Colber's gates. Perhaps their numbers intimidated the Gnolls nearby. The strategy of an ambush to unsuspecting riders on their way home seemed too clever for Gnolls, but there they were, standing and braced in mass—lined up as an elite army and blocking the path. Lady Sheen ordered her riders to halt, seeing how the Gnolls had not only blocked them from the path to Colber but also the way to retreat.

Colber is a fortress that lies just northwest of two lakes, almost the exact center of Essend's kingdom. The riders were between the two lakes of Colber with the fortresses' high towers in view. Lady Sheen knew that the city watch had already noticed the massing of the Gnoll force set along the rolling hills. Her only thought was to get the ones she found to the safety of the walls before the king compassionately made a rash decision. She was his daughter after all.

Though the way was blocked, it did appear the Gnolls were misguided in their belief that they could stop even a few Primitive Riders charging them head-on. Some Gnolls leaped at the riders sitting atop their Primitive Banes, but the mighty beasts swatted them away while keeping stride. As the riders broke through the Gnolls' lines, leading to Colber, some of the riders were lost protecting Lady Sheen and the others who carried the young casters and the Goblins.

At this time, what should be known about the loyalty of a Primitive Bane to its rider is it is a bond unlike any other. A Primitive Bane will spend hours at the side of their fallen rider. Should the enemy still be in view, they become enraged and wildly slaughter whatever they can lay their hands on. And after the dust settles, should they not be slain, they find their rider on the battlefield again, holding them in their arms until they starve to death. When the rider dies, so does the Primitive Bane.

Seeing their masters fall, they now beat their fists into one Gnoll after another, even biting with their mighty jaws to render limbs from them. But the Gnolls didn't retreat, nor did they back down. While the Gnolls may have failed to stop all the riders from getting through, they managed to slay seven and soon overwhelmed their Primitive Banes with sheer numbers.

Avaleigh looked up seeing they were through the horde of Gnolls, now chasing them. Her eyes turned toward the approaching gates of Colber and gasped—realizing she had seen the gates before.

14
Best Laid Plans

"I know these gates," Avaleigh said to her brother when they were safely inside the city walls. A portcullis cranked noisily to the ground just after the towering doors closed behind them. "Remember the vision I spoke of back in the old caster's wheat field, the one from the Tremor of Power?"

Hayden thought for a moment and then became wide-eyed letting out a large sigh.

"Gnolls are the army?" He asked with a tone of disbelief.

"I'm afraid so," Avaleigh sighed. Her memory recalled the vision that appeared in her mind, and she searched to recall any specific details about the vision. Yet, there was nothing—just the gate, and an army of shadowy figures marching against it.

"Wait," she said. "I remember the army being great, but they were hidden. It was like darkness covered them. I wonder if they will attack tonight."

"We are counting on it," Lady Sheen stepped in. "Gnolls are most dangerous at night due to their uncanny ability to see in the dark."

As the young casters were about to inquire of Colber's defenses, a familiar face stepped out into the light, a wild reddish beard streaked in silver, long locks of much the same, and a welcoming grin to Avaleigh and Hayden who did not expect to see him. It was their father's brother and head caster of Holprice, Uncle Timothy. His heavy build tossed a looming shadow over the two as he leaned on his caster's staff, a dark stained wood that ran straight up and twisted around toward the top. The head of his staff reached just past his head and carved into the face of a gaping lion with outstretched carnivorous bird wings protruding out the back of its mane—surprisingly something the two young casters had never seen before.

"You did not expect to see me," their uncle chuckled.

"Are you angry with us?" Avaleigh's words carried a touch of shame.

"No," her uncle replied gently. "I knew the time had come. I knew you two would be so bold to go looking for your father and mother, and the secret book your father was looking for. The thing is, I too have been in search of it, for him and your mother as well."

"How did you get here ahead of us?" Hayden asked.

"I have other means of travel," Uncle Timothy grinned, but then his face grew grim. He stared just to the right of Hayden's left shoulder, sensing something amiss. The air around his nephew had become unfamiliar to him, not that he could quite understand, but he felt another presence lingering unseen.

Uncle Timothy told the young casters and the Goblins to follow him. Walking through the streets of Colber, and on up into the fortress keep, allowed Avaleigh to take notice of Colber's strength. Its walls were fortified with large brick and mortar with four main high towers in each corner. She had noticed coming in that the outer walls were barricaded by sharpened pikes along the bottom and a moat that flowed in from the two lakes. Another sight revealed several stables housing and caring for Primitive Banes much like one would for horses, but appeared more like an enormous chicken coop with nests stacked one on top of the other.

Hayden noticed the large piles of what he could recognize as feces and no doubt from the Primitive Banes. He remained puzzled, though, noticing that his nostrils were not burning from any sort of horrific stench.

"It surprised me too the first time I came here," Grug said, seeing the boy in a bit of shock at just how much dung was piled high in front of him. "But it's true. Primitive Bane feces is the top commodity of Colber. It's practically odorless, makes good mortar, which fetches a wealthy price in trade throughout the four kingdoms."

"You said practically odorless," Hayden replied. "What do you mean practically?"

"Well," Grug confessed. "When a Primitive Bane's feces carry an odor, then you know they're ill. And when a Primitive Bane is ill, the commodity as it were is compromised, and needs to be disposed of quickly due to its pungency."

"How pungent?" Hayden grinned, keeping his curiosity going, and hoping to gain more ammunition for insults later on.

"It could yank a Blighttalon right out of the sky," Grug laughed and was soon joined by the boy.

"Keep up now," Uncle Timothy hurried. "I know piles of poo are hilarious to young boys…and Goblins. But don't fall behind."

"Isn't your favorite joke about a man named John who visits the John?" Avaleigh asked, her stare held a judgmental raised eyebrow.

"Yes," Uncle Timothy replied. "But that is high-cheek humor?

"Funny, I thought the John was a place for the lower cheeks," Hayden teased with a chuckle as he stepped lightly toward his uncle. "I will say that is one of my favorites you tell—the John confesses his love for John saying 'My love for you is in a state of dysentery…I can't hold it in.'"

Uncle Timothy blurted out a laugh, which was followed by the rest joining him. The atmosphere felt a bit lighter despite the circumstances of a Gnoll army united and gathering outside the fortress. Their laughter soon dwindled once the door to the palace swung open, revealing the immaculately embroidered tapestries drooping down from the walls and ceiling. Each one carried the emblem and colors of the Essend—the famed golden stag on sapphire, highlighted in black.

Just as Hayden entered the palace, Jasper's form became visible. His uncle stepped toward the specter, examining its face and shape.

"This is bound to you, yes?" He asked Hayden. "How did this happen?"

Hayden began to speak of the scroll to his uncle until a guard interrupted, urging them to see the king.

"We shall speak on this later," Uncle Timothy said, gently squeezing Hayden's shoulder to let the lad know he did not need to stress about his concern.

Tradition dictates that each king who takes the throne of Essend shall carry on the name "Colber," whether they be born from the bloodline or adopt the name should they marry into the royalty, leaving behind the name given them at birth. Thus, King Colber the VI was once a man by the name of Gladale and married the daughter of the previous king. She sat by his side, equally powerful in her authority, but more so—she was also a caster, specifically a master in Allay. Queen Zoie had been her given name, but she had earned the epithet "Grace of Essend," in growing to learn the fourth step in Allay casting.

Unlike all other magic, Allay casting is learned and taught in three steps. Attempting a spell before the step before is mastered can bring disastrous results ending in outcomes such as permanent damage or even death. The first two steps focus on healing oneself.

Heal Shell allows a caster to heal their skin of cuts, bruises, and any other abrasions. "Heal Brawn" allows a caster to focus on their muscle injuries and fatigue.

Heal Frame allows a caster to focus on their bones, marrow, and cartilage.

Finally, the last step includes a spell known as Heal Matter, allowing the caster to not only heal themselves but essentially anything or anyone. Learning the final step is rare as not many who practice Allay magic can master it within their lifetime. Queen Zoie—The Grace of Essend—was one deviating and young exception.

While her husband had become known for his brilliant strategic mind, Queen Zoie held a high intellect in understanding how Allay magic works and contributed to Shroe's once-proud library of knowledge. Avaleigh assumed it was one of the many possible reasons her face appeared so grim upon the girl entering the room with the others. Assuredly, it wasn't all about losing Shroe to the horde of Gnolls. Jasper drew every eye to him as they approached the king and queen's throne.

Avaleigh didn't stare directly into the queen's almond-shaped eyes as they drew closer. However, the queen's voice held a welcoming tone and helped the girl take a sigh of relief.

"I see one of you is cursed," Queen Zoie observed before the king could utter any sort of greeting.

"I agree," Hayden bravely spoke up.

"It does seem to be the biggest elephant in the room," Uncle Timothy scratched his chin.

His remark made the king chuckle, opening the rest of the full room of lords and ladies to enjoy a small laugh, tearing down any uncomfortable tension that there was, in fact, a specter hovering just behind Hayden.

"I was about to inquire of the boy about how this came to pass," Uncle Timothy confessed. "Yet the guard summoned us to come swiftly to speak with you before I could learn anything."

"Well, it's not the first time I've seen a ghost haunt someone," King Colber admitted, his face returning to a sterner appearance. "I would also like to hear of how such a thing happened to the boy. But now is not the time to investigate."

"Agreed, my lord," Uncle Timothy replied.

"Undoubtedly, you're aware of the horde of Gnolls lurking outside my castle," the king continued. "I would attack them head-on with the full force of our Primitive Riders, however, I have estimated they would still overwhelm us."

"What do you propose?" Uncle Timothy asked.

"I do not think it will be long before they siege Colber, and still overrun us," the king sighed, yet remained composed. "We will need your casting abilities and those of your two little ones. You've told me much about their progress. I long to see what they can do for the Kingdom of Essend."

"I knew they would not fail to reach Colber," Uncle Timothy grinned at both the young casters. "Our abilities are at your command. Yet I insist these two remain behind the walls to defend the city. I do not believe they are ready to take on such numbers."

"No one will be leaving the defense of the walls," the king reassured. "My strategy is simple. We let the Gnolls overrun the walls and funnel into the first courtyard. From there, we spring our trap."

"I am intrigued," Uncle Timothy admitted. "What do you need us to do?"

Once the king explained his strategy, the two young casters and Goblins followed Uncle Timothy up one of the large towers to take their post.

"Are you the Elder Caster of Colber as well as Holprice? Hayden directed his question toward his uncle.

"No," Uncle Timothy replied. "Queen Zoie is the Elder Caster of Colber. I simply provide counsel from time to time."

"How did you get here so fast again?" Avaleigh spun a more curious inquiry.

"One day, you will know," Uncle Timothy sighed, but with a smile that made Avaleigh believe the day was not far off.

15

When the Gnolls Go Marching

King Colber the VI correctly assumed the time of the Gnolls' siege. While still a mystery as to how the tribes became unified, such thoughts were shoved aside in seeing the Gnoll horde gather in the thousands outside the city walls, standing shoulder to shoulder as dusk settled and storm clouds brewed above. The skies cracked and thundered, sending down rain almost as strong as the ocean's tides.

The army of Gnolls began to spread out in a "U" shape, with the middle of the horde standing in line with Colber's main gate. Why they did not fully surround the castle is simple—the backside of the fortress held a strategic element almost right up to its wall, a marshland stretching for about a mile, holding various points with unforgiving soil that could swallow the weight of a Gnoll whole year-round. Even Primitive Riders had to venture around the marshland should they travel north into Gombder Forest.

Now, every Gnoll's footsteps grew louder as they broke into a faster pace, splashing through muddy puddles, and recklessly howling while charging Colber's walls. They brought with them long tree trunks, bracing them against the fortress walls and taking turns climbing to reach the top. Many of them were now over the wall, standing confused. Not one arrow flew in their direction, not even as they were charging. There were strange, thick layers of ice blocking the doors to the fortress towers. Thus, they found the stairs that led down into the courtyard. Soon more and more funneled into it, every one of them sniffing the air, searching for flesh to rip apart. The way to Colber's keep was also blocked by thick layers of ice except for its center gate.

Gnolls are not usually the type of beasts to panic. However, being packed tightly in a courtyard with nowhere to run can be a reason to do so when lightning strikes several into an instant state of demise. It was the signal for the rest of Colber's trap to be sprung. Archers popped up from the fortress towers, as they did from the wall of the keep. Hundreds of arrows suddenly sang their way through the air and into the courtyard, hitting their marks. Many more Gnolls landed against the mucky cobblestone never to rise again. Another volley soon followed, and another, and another.

Uncle Timothy surveyed from one of the keep towers with the two young casters and the three Goblins. Despite monster blood being spilled in the courtyard—something a typical nine-year-old boy would plead to watch—Hayden was fidgeting with the violet fragments that he acquired.

"How does one concentrate with all that noise?" Hayden huffed. The remark brought a puzzled look to his sister's face, as it did to his uncle.

"Tell me more about your…Jasper is what you called the specter?"

Uncle Timothy stepped away from watching the fray.

"I've pretty much told you everything I know already," the boy replied. "I read some funny words from a scroll we won in an insult contest in Lem. The next morning, Jasper was there and has been following me around ever since. I ended up getting nulled out when we were fighting some Ash Hounds, and then Jasper brought me back to life. I can see pretty much the way he sees now—so much blue. And more recently, I am able to see what he sees. It's quite simple."

"If I may interject," Jasper floated in between the two. "I didn't mean to be a curse upon your nephew. I sincerely hope he remains living. I hope there are no harsh feelings toward me."

"You are a chatty curse, aren't you?" Uncle Timothy rolled his eyes. "It has nothing to do with your will, specter. The words of the scroll are what I care about, which may be the only way to know how to put your spirit to rest and free my nephew from what could be a worse fate than death."

"What do you mean?" His uncle's words nabbed Hayden's attention.

"I will not hide anything from you, boy," Uncle Timothy knelt and placed his hands on Hayden's shoulders, staring straight into his eyes. "I've seen what this manner of casting can do to someone. Haunt is a conjuring cast, but it is rarely used and has likely only been used by Witches of the Wilds. That's why here in Essend, we don't focus on conjuring. We leave that to folks in Autumnwich."

"Do you know someone else who is cursed by Sight of the Dead?" Avaleigh asked.

"I do," Uncle Timothy admitted. "But that is a story for another time. Right now, we need to help clear the courtyard."

"I would if I could figure out how to combine these fragments," Hayden pressed. "I want to see it light up my new staff."

"Did Argus give those to you?" Uncle Timothy asked.

"Yes," Avaleigh responded excitedly. "How did you know?"

"Well, I gave them to him a while back," Uncle Timothy replied. "I told him they might come in handy if he ever had casters under his command. Yet, he's not a huge fan of magic. Makes him somewhat nervous."

"Are you going to help me or not?" Hayden bellowed out. "I thought we needed to start killing some Gnolls."

Uncle Timothy grinned at his nephew. Without a word, he reached out and slowly pulled the stone fragments away from Hayden. In a small, concentrated casting of Thunder Strike, he held the fragments together, and they suddenly fused back together.

"Casting stones are very special," he explained. "In order to restore any shattered pieces, one must highly focus the same spell on the stone fragments the stone is desiring to cast."

Hayden excitedly plucked the fused stone from his uncle's hands. He held his eyes wide open with an almost sinister smirk that did not go unnoticed by Avaleigh or his uncle. The violet stone burst forth with sparks of lightning as if it were gripping the head of Hayden's staff. He jumped to his feet, waving it in the air. Electric charges swarmed up and down Hayden's arms in hues of violet, blue, and suddenly bright red. Uncle Timothy, Avaleigh, and the three Goblins gawked at the boy who now surged with so much power that they each took a step back. Even the archers along the tower moved aside when Hayden approached the wall.

Lightning swirled all around him now, charging into hues of magenta and then green. The boy's body began trembling as the hues again changed, becoming bright white, and no other colors could be seen. Hayden's eyes lit up. With the immensity of his power enveloped, he peered upward. The skies above cracked with lightning and one struck his staff. In a single moment, Hayden let loose a force of Thunder Strike that Uncle Timothy admittedly had never seen.

Hayden's newly enhanced power was not only his doing. His uncle also noticed the amulet he wore, as it was being pulled into the electro-magnetic force. Hayden's cast of Thunder Strike struck so powerfully, yet so controlled that none of the electrical streams hit anything other than Gnolls. Almost in an instant, the cast cleared the courtyard, and the Gnolls that were still outside the walls turned and fled.

When the calm came, all eyes on the tower were still fixated on Hayden, who didn't even appear to be fatigued by the amount of energy he exuded. It's what Hayden felt, but not exactly what the others witnessed. The boy breathed out and fell backward into his uncle's arms. His eyes had already rolled into death. Once more, Jasper drew near him, reaching down into his chest, and pumping his heart back to life. For one so young to have so much power and one who was bound to a curse of the dead, it frightened Uncle Timothy to his very core. Despite Hayden's control of the power that he cast; the boy had killed himself in the process. And Uncle Timothy began pondering how he should have stopped him.

The boy enjoyed the praises of the king and queen, seeing how none of their troops were lost. The large body count of the Gnolls dead in the courtyard was only a fraction of their true numbers. However, if the Gnolls believed a powerful caster stood against them in Colber, they would likely not try another siege for quite some time.

Hayden appeared unaware that he perished again, bringing Uncle Timothy to ponder even more, as perhaps it held a clue to the origins of the curse. The boy did not deny dying, but he remained unconcerned with his demise—until his uncle reminded him of the consequences once more.

"Each time you die, Hayden, you become drawn ever more into the shadow," Uncle Timothy urged. "You must hold back your power to not destroy yourself."

"I didn't mean to," Hayden said, with tears running down his cheeks. "I just wanted to take care of the Gnolls so we could leave to find father and mother."

"Tell me more about this curse," Uncle Timothy said, placing his arms around the boy. "Tell me what it feels like. Tell me what it felt like to wield so much power. Tell me as much as you can."

They moved the conversation to a more private room in the keep after Avaleigh withdrew the solidified water shields from all the entrances. Her uncle noticed that it was not difficult for her, something only Master Casters could perform—commanding water to melt into vapor.

"Their power has immaculately grown," he thought. "I wish to not leave them alone."

Uncle Timothy led the way into a quiet study in the keep, sitting the young casters down in cushy linen chairs next to a warm fire. The room's long drapes were drawn, creating a hush of shadows around the light of the fireplace. Uncle Timothy placed a kettle of water on a hook and nestled it over the flames.

"Oh, how I wish I could taste tea again," Jasper softly whined above Hayden's left shoulder.

"Why don't you come down next to Hayden?" Uncle Timothy invited. "Perhaps you may be of help to us in understanding this curse."

Delighted by the hospitality, Jasper floated down and hovered slightly above the cushion of the chair next to the boy. Avaleigh and Hayden waited quietly while their uncle sat back, his hand stroking his long, red beard. Before he could speak, he noticed Grug and the two twin Goblins enter the room. While Goblins do not care for tea, they do love soft furniture for their hindquarters. The three pulled up more of the cushy chairs near the fire, the twins sharing a wide-based seat.

"I suppose Grug and these two should hear our conversation," Uncle Timothy said. "I know you are seeking your father and mother, yet I also know you are seeking the book of secret casting."

"We cannot hide anything from you," Avaleigh admitted.

"Yet something was hidden from you," Uncle Timothy confessed. "I permitted you two venturing out to come here. I knew it would test your abilities. And since we are no longer keeping secrets, I have a couple to tell you."

"What do you mean?" Hayden asked. "What secrets do you have?"

"I made sure you would find your way here, with the help of some others," Uncle Timothy explained. "You received those amulets from an old caster friend of mine, Dolber. I swore Grug to silence, but it was I who commissioned him to find you along the road and to help protect you until you made it here. I also informed Lady Sheen of your whereabouts so that she would ride out to bring you here."

"How did you know where we were?" Avaleigh demanded.
"That is the one secret I must keep for now," Uncle Timothy replied. "I will show you in time. For now, I can see that the two of you have overcome much with Grug's help. However, I cannot impress upon

Grug further to assist you anymore."

"It is no burden," Grug interjected. "My family is with me."

"What do you mean that your family is with you?" Hayden vocalized somewhat surprisingly loudly.

"Morlo and Porlo are Grug's sons," Uncle Timothy explained.

Grug continued to express how he longed to be on an extended quest again, and how he wanted his sons to see the world. As young warriors, they would learn much, and Grug admitted he found it fortunate that Timothy had given him the chance to do so.

"Don't you have a wife?" Avaleigh exclaimed. "What about her?"

"Goblins are not like humans," Grug replied. "Mates only remain together for a season to breed their bloodline. I have not done so in many years. Several of my bloodlines are fully grown."

"What of Morlo and Porlo?" Avaleigh kept up her concern.

"What does that matter?" Hayden tried to cease what he believed to be pointless jabber.

"Their instinct to fight is greater than having a mate," Grug pressed onward despite Hayden's huffs of disinterest. "We shall see in time."

"I respect your willingness to remain with my kin, Grug," Uncle

Timothy said. "We shall see to it you're better equipped before departure. However, as for this curse that is upon Hayden—this was something I did not intend. I truly wish you still had the scroll."

"Is it on a piece of paper like this?" A gruff stuttering tone fell from Porlo's mouth. He pulled a small of rolled-up paper from the small pouch on his belt. "I go back into the boy's room before leaving, cause I want scented flowers. They smell good. I see a scrap of paper on the bed. I grabbed it in case we had nothing to start a fire."

"When did you have time to do that?" Hayden asked, completely surprised.

"Porlo sneaky," Morlo snickered. "Porlo likes to steal more than kill."

"Not true!" Porlo growled.

"Cease this at once!" Uncle Timothy shouted. "Give it here!"

The Behemoth King of Gombder

Nothing appeared extraordinary about the scroll as Uncle Timothy held it in his hand. He pulled it toward the light of the fire to see if the words of the scroll would reappear. He moved the piece of paper closer to the heart, wondering if perhaps the words on the scroll were simply written with lemon juice. Still, nothing reappeared. He sighed heavily, seemingly lost to how the mystery would be solved.

"What if the words were transferred somehow?" Avaleigh surmised. "What if Jasper became the manifestation of the words? So, it is reasonable that his aura should reveal them."

"Thinking just like your father, eh?" Uncle Timothy grinned. "He must have spoken with you about curses before."

"Some," the girl replied. "More specifically, he did speak to me several times about the manifestations of curses, and how they are likely the root of uncovering the origins."

Uncle Timothy motioned for Jasper to draw closer to him and held up the scroll to the specter's transparent body. A faint glow began on the slip at first, but soon the words came alive in a shimmering, blue flame that struck the text back into focus. Though Uncle Timothy admitted he saw the words; he did not say them aloud. The words read:

"Hto yakjo ew eno jtupp zoyequo hto yakjo ew hto ehtok. Huro toox inhe jpaquzok unx hto yakjo jtupp kijo he onyaquzok."

"These words are written from a Witch of the Wilds," Uncle Timothy said. "I will not read them aloud as they are, but I can translate what it says—The curse of one shall become the curse of the other. Take heed into slumber and the curse shall rise to encumber."

"Jasper was cursed as a Bonecrackle, uncle," Avaleigh pointed out.

"I am not pleased with what I did," Jasper quickly interjected. "I became overwhelmed with grief. I cast a spell to destroy myself to gain the power to kill those who slew my family. I was already mortally wounded and believed becoming undead would be swift. Though, I changed into something I did not expect."

"I understand the urges Hayden has now," Uncle Timothy sighed, sitting back in his chair. "What Jasper sought was power, and to do so, he would harm himself. So, now we know the symptoms of the curse. But the origin took place while Hayden slept."

"Do I just need to sleep again?" Hayden ignorantly concocted. "Maybe this time, I could do something different."

"To undo a curse, usually the opposite is required," Uncle Timothy confessed. "Which would mean, Jasper needs to sleep. But specters never slumber. This curse is crafty, indeed."

"How is it you can translate what the scroll says?" Avaleigh's words dripped with curiosity.

"Your father and I grew up in an interesting time and place," Uncle Timothy replied. "We do not originally hail from Holprice, though our titles as casters make that claim. Before dedicating our lives as casters to the monastery of Holprice, we were both children of Byre—the only haven in Essend where Witches of the Wilds wish to remain at peace with the king."

"You're a Witch of the Wilds?!" Avaleigh gasped. "And father too?!"

"Once upon a time," Uncle Timothy admitted. "But we did not follow the shrewd bitterness as many of our kin did. Many years ago, there was a great separation in Byre, one that almost came to bloodshed had it not been for Queen Zoie's grandfather, King Colber the IV. He made a pact with many Witches of the Wilds, and many of us even left to seek haven elsewhere in Shroe, Holprice, and Remel as casters. We brought our knowledge with us, a priceless asset to the monasteries—such as knowledge in Allay casting and even Conjuring. When your father met your mother in Holprice, I knew it would become our new home."

"I can't believe our father's a Witch," Hayden gawked. "And our uncle, who we've known all our life, is a Witch."

"Not anymore," Uncle Timothy corrected. "Our bloodline mixed with your ancient bloodline could be the reason why you grow powerful more easily than most. As young casters, and my kin under my care, I charge you not to dispel what I've told you to anyone. I know the both of you would come to find out eventually. But should anyone learn of your origins, your lives could be in more danger than they are right now."

"What do you mean?" Avaleigh asked.

"Your mother and your father have gone missing because of the book we seek," Uncle Timothy explained. "I knew one day the both of you would go looking for them, and the book. But there is much danger that surrounds such a thing. And while I would have preferred to seek both of them out on my own, I know it is not possible. So, here we are."

"I'm glad," Hayden's smile became infectious to his uncle. "Here we are."

Uncle Timothy led the young casters and the Goblins to the king's armory after they finished their tea in somewhat of a time of silence as Hayden enjoyed slurping his beverage more than enjoying the stillness.

The king and queen met them with a blessing to take whatever they needed for their quest ahead. Uncle Timothy first clasped a band around Hayden's wrist, something he referred to as an enchanted restraint. Essentially, such a wristband was used specifically for powerful casters to not overload themselves and prevent the caster from accumulating too much power that would kill them. It was exactly what Hayden needed to keep him from destroying himself and to preserve his power under control, however, he did not take a liking to it and almost cursed his uncle for tricking him and locking the band to his wrist.

"The only person who can unlock this is the one who put it on," Uncle Timothy bent down to meet Hayden's glare. "So, you best put that death stare away because you'll never get it off if you kill me."

Avaleigh could see her brother's eyes were not his own, but the curse that defied the deed. His eyes were shimmering silver and blue, and when he pushed his gaze toward her, she did her best to reassure him that the wristband would likely not affect his power much, as he was already casting extremely powerful spells before the curse. The boy did not appear to care for the flattery at first, but after a few moments rolled his eyes and giggled.

While the Goblins plundered through weapons of some of the most finely crafted axes, bows, and armor, the king charged Uncle Timothy with a small quest—to journey to Dundlen and send back word about the messengers he sent there. Both men knew it was likely Gnolls that could have slain the few he sent, but the king also desired to know the affairs of Dundlen and how the citadel fared.

Grug returned to the view of Uncle Timothy and the king and queen. He appeared pleased with the prize he found among the armory—dark-plated armor that fit his bulky body almost perfectly, coupled with a helm that would make a Goblin chieftain envious. The openings for the eyes were wide and elegantly shaped into the faceguard which protruded small spikey studs. The brim of the helm smoothly curved back over his head, but held a long and narrow spike attached to the brow. Around the brim was a band of gold with inlaid polished stones almost as dark as the helm's plating.

"That helm once belonged to my father," the king pointed out. "I feel that it will do better with you than sitting around in here."

"It is a mighty gift," Grug replied. "I thank you for your generosity, and I am most honored to wear a helm fit for a king such as your father."

The bulky Goblin also acquired new throwing axes that held dust from years of hanging upon a weapon rack in a dimly lit corner. Yet the metal caught Grug's eyes, as it was good and strong, and light as a feather to him. He fashioned a belt of which the king did not know of its origin, but it held the six new throwing axes with room for at least two more. Since Grug favored the axes he already carried, he was delighted that the handles could fit through the two remaining loops of the belt. His favorite find, however, was a double-sided axe with a piercing point at both ends. The long handle still held a polished shine, wrapped in beautiful black leather. Its blade revealed etched markings unknown to him.

"This axe is old," the king sighed with a tone of awe, seeing the Goblin present it to him and asking him about the markings. "I do believe this belonged to a Primitive Rider, one under the first King of Colber. Primitive Riders don't use such a weapon anymore. But these markings are the name the rider gave his weapon—"Gnoll Gobbler." It's written in the tongue of the Gnolls. They likely know this weapon.

Morlo and Porlo had replaced their hunting bows with matching longbows made of dark pine with silver-plated birds wrapped along the curvature of the wood at both ends. Their quiver of arrows had also doubled, and doubled still, as both carried another with them along with the ones they strapped to their backs. Each quiver easily held forty arrows. The only new armor they donned was a spiked shoulder plate, again matching one another—Morlo wore the one fitted to his left, while Porlo wore the one fitted to his right. They said nothing when they presented their findings to the king.

"Those are bows meant for elite archers," Queen Zoie spoke. "Not many can master pulling back such a strong string and aim it with pristine accuracy."

Morlo looked confused at Porlo and then pulled an arrow from one of the quivers. There were targets down on the far end of the armory—the king's private shooting range—and Morlo swiftly placed an arrow into the bow, and drew it back as if pulling on a piece of string. He let the arrow fly and it sailed straight into one of the targets over a hundred paces away. The king and queen were both taken aback by the feat, and both watched Porlo draw his bow back with ease, letting an arrow fly. The Goblin's arrow landed somewhat closer to the center of the target Morlo had just hit. And Porlo let out a scoffing snivel to his brother. Morlo didn't look at him but stormed away.

"I assume they both got some great shots in from the tower," Queen Zoie said to Uncle Timothy. "I had no idea Goblins could be such excellent archers."

"They're different," Grug interjected and then followed after Morlo, followed by Porlo.

"The Goblins are finished," Uncle Timothy said, now focusing on the two young casters. "What does your armory hold for two young casters?"

Queen Zoie smiled and bid they follow her. Unto Avaleigh and Hayden, the queen bestowed an enchanted cloak to ward against grievous weather: in snowstorms, it would warm their bodies; in severe heat, it would cool them down. And in torrential rains, it would help keep them dry. Unto Uncle Timothy, she slipped him a thin-bound leather book. He thumbed to the title page on the inside and suddenly closed it.

"Many thanks to you both," Uncle Timothy smiled at the king and queen.

There were still thunderous clouds overhead when the new day dawned. Uncle Timothy stood just outside Colber's walls accompanied by the two young casters, and the three Goblins. Their gaze turned toward the West, Gombder Forest, and beyond that, Ogrin Forest—two treacherous places filled undoubtedly with scattered Gnolls and other monsters yet to be faced. Beyond them was their destination, Dundlen, and from there to Byre to try and find a way to free Hayden from his curse. Yet, they would not be going alone.

Lady Sheen brought forth with her three Primitive Banes, all three bound to her. She commanded one to let the three Goblins ride it and to the other Uncle Timothy and Hayden. Avaleigh would ride with her. The Primitive Banes began to march, and the sounds of another storm brewing cracked in the distant skies. Soon, rain would come again.

The haze among the trees rolled in more eerie than usual and the cluster of clouds above took shape as if to mock the travelers riding upon Primitive Banes into the neighboring forest along Colber's western front. When the rain began to weave its way down, it became greeted by a biting wind—something unusual for spring near Colber. The chilling sting didn't appear to bother the enormous beasts. Some of their riders knew how to ignore being drenched for a time. Yet the two young casters, despite their weather cloaks, still felt the nasty sharp wind upon the napes of their necks. Their feet clenched tightly into the saddle as they shivered and covered their heads with the hoods of their cloaks.

Goblins are much different in the rain. Despite it being one of the very few times they bathe, their enjoyment of being wet is mostly childlike and playful—such as lifting their mouths toward the heavens, sticking out their tongues, and trying to catch the drops as they fall. Morlo stretched out just a bit too much that he tumbled off the Primitive Bane landing face-first into the mucky grime of Gombder's marshland. His brother, Porlo, scoffed at his clumsiness, and soon his laughter became infectious to the young casters.

"We cannot tarry here," Lady Sheen was quick to double back as Grug pulled his son from the muck. "Gombder is not a forgiving place."

The forest does well to shroud many things that dwell there. Its trees are massively broad and tall, making it so even big things can hide like small things. And what Lady Sheen held an edge about was something she only faced once before. The monster in her mind kept her eyes darting, as she knew it unlikely to believe it would catch the scent of Goblin flesh. Gombder was her least favorite place to travel. She whispered to Avaleigh that she would rather face the army of Gnolls once more than go against the monster that dwelt in the forest.

"If such a monster exists, and is such a threat, shouldn't we destroy it given a chance," Avaleigh's logical thoughts became spoken aloud. "What can outmatch a Primitive Bane?"

"A Behemoth Toad," Lady Sheen answered. But it wasn't just her words. The haze of the forest began to dissipate, and there the monster sat upon the road dead ahead—a massive amphibian, and more specifically of the toad variety.

BEHEMOTH TOAD

"What did you do? Summon the thing?" Uncle Timothy poked Lady Sheen.

It wasn't moving, just squatting in the way. Its big yellow eyes blinked several times while staring directly at the travelers. Its muck-green skin excreted a jelly mucus that smelt similar to that of rotting eggs while its white underbelly periodically and sporadically inflated and then deflated.

"How is that threat?" Hayden chimed in. "It appears more like a brainless mutt to me."

"Don't be fooled," Uncle Timothy shot a quick retort. "We're likely just far enough away. If it's hungry, it will lurch its tongue out like a whip and nab you."

"The only thing is it doesn't need to wrap around you," Lady Sheen added. "Its tongue holds an adhesive compound that sticks to just about anything. You'd be gone in the blink of an eye."

"Wait a minute," Hayden interjected. "I'm no animal expert, but I remember frogs have sticky tongues. Toads don't. So, either this thing is more like a frog than a toad, and whoever said this was like a toad doesn't know their amphibians."

"Are you seriously arguing this right now? Avaleigh shot her brother a scowl. "There's a giant monster sitting on the road and we're here wondering if we're going to be its breakfast or not."

"If you're so concerned about it Avaleigh, why don't you just blow it away with your Stormy Gale?" Hayden shot back.

"Enough!" Uncle Timothy uttered out his frustration. "Keep your voices down."

However, another sound approached, one that portrayed a team of horses and cartwheels—four teams to be exact carrying soldiers and supplies. Their fortune became destitute as they rounded the bend and the Behemoth Toad rapidly spun around and shot forth its tongue toward one of the horses. The cart shattered to pieces as it slammed into the toad's stalky and plump body. The rest of the caravan halted altogether. There were enough moments of silence for the members of the caravan to hear the crunching of horse bones. The soldiers and driver of the first cart lay still, presumed dead upon impact.

"We have no choice," Uncle Timothy said. "Those are soldiers from Dundlen. We attack."

Lady Sheen did not appear pleased to charge in, but she followed Uncle Timothy's lead as Hayden wildly exclaimed his excitement as the Primitive Bane took off toward the Behemoth. Grug remained much more hesitant, knowing full well that the creature had a particular taste for Goblin flesh.

"Shoot out its eyes," he told Morlo and Porlo as he squeezed his knees into the Primitive Bane. He directed the beast at full speed to run in circles around the Behemoth Toad, knowing they would be spotted and most likely be targeted first for the monster's next meal. And he sped the Primitive Bane passed the other two who were dangerously charging the monster head-on.

The Toad became easily convinced to give chase to the Goblins riding around it. Grug knew that if he could keep the Primitive Bane moving fast enough, the Behemoth would have no time to properly shoot out its tongue to reel them in—it desperately tried though, taking major leaps and strides to keep up with the primate beast carrying Goblin meat. With the Behemoth distracted, Lady Sheen and Uncle Timothy went to help the caravanners from Dundlen, pulling several injured soldiers from the muck of the marsh.

Morlo and Porlo positioned themselves, Morlo holding Porlo in the saddle while the better shot took aim. Porlo let loose his first arrow just as Grug turned the Primitive Bane, dodging not only a tree but the tongue of the monster behind them. Porlo's arrow spun effortlessly and plunged into the left eye of the Behemoth Toad, erupting a greenish substance that continued to spray fervently and dismantled its yellowish glow. Grug was surprised the monster had ceased chasing him. He returned to the others, seeing the enormous Toad still in view. The monster gradually made its way back toward the caravan.

"It's smart," Grug told Uncle Timothy. "I've fought several before, and they always become enraged when being shot in the eye."

"Goblins are clever creatures," Uncle Timothy admitted. "But this one is not falling for it."

The caster's gaze remained on the Behemoth that now ceased its approach. He was not aware that Hayden had dropped to the ground and had begun to summon a Thunder Strike spell, amassing his power.

"Something isn't right," Uncle Timothy remarked.

Moments later another horse got snatched from a cart, a long, sticky tongue wrapping around the terrified equine, which also yanked the whole cart with its soldiers toward the owner of the enormous tongue. The sound of bones crunching resounded from the mist and fog. It caught everyone's attention, which made soldiers jump out of their carts—the only two remaining. Uncle Timothy turned and noticed Hayden.

"Avaleigh!" He shouted. "Blow away the fog."

The young caster swiftly summoned her Stormy Gale, pushing the fog and mist away to reveal an even more enormous Toad monster, twice the size of the other Behemoth Toad, but with dark red eyes, and glistening violet skin.

"The Behemoth King of Gombder," Uncle Timothy muttered under his breath.

"Fire arrows upon the beast," one of the soldiers bravely spurted out. "We will not die without a fight!"

Hayden looked up at his uncle who met his gaze.

"Kill it," Uncle Timothy said. "Give it everything you have. Now!"

Hayden let loose an electrical charge that clapped a thunderous echo as he released it from his being. The lightning enshrouded the King Behemoth, striking it in various places all over its body. Several arrows followed the blast, some hitting their targets, but the Behemoth didn't even budge. The monster appeared unphased by the lightning that had struck it, and the arrows did little to pierce its blubbery mass to do any sort of vital damage.

"Keep calm everyone," Uncle Timothy commanded. "Nobody moves! Trust me."

Whether courage or fright gripped them, every soldier remained where they were. Even the Primitive Banes didn't shift, or make much of a sound. The two Behemoth Toads began to wander off and soon disappeared into the forest. Hayden shot his uncle a wide expression of confusion but only received a smile in return.

"Greetings," Uncle Timothy bid the soldiers welcome. "I assume you are coming from Dundlen."

"Arwal, actually," spoke up the soldier who had commanded his troops to fire on the Behemoth. "We are indeed soldiers of Dundlen, though. What interest do you have there?"

"We were sent to seek what had happened to the messengers my father, King Colber, sent there," Lady Sheen interjected.

"Lady Sheen," the soldier gasped, and quickly bent his knee. The others followed. "I was not aware it was you. Please forgive me."

"We do not have time for formalities," Lady Sheen explained. "What of the messengers we sent? Have you received them?"

"Yes, my lady," the soldier replied. "This was a caravan of supplies to aid Colber. It's the quickest we could muster. We were moving with haste, but as you can see, we ran into trouble. Thanks to you, half the supplies survived."

"Has Dundlen had trouble with the Gnolls recently?" Uncle Timothy inquired.

"Mostly small war parties, nothing more," the soldier explained. "When we received word there was an army of them on Colber's doorstep, we did the best we could."

"Why do so few soldiers come with the caravan?" Uncle Timothy continued.

The soldier continued to explain that the only soldiers Dundlen could send were infantry. Cavalry couldn't be spared as it's much easier to kill a Gnoll in the open when riding a mount. Thus the infantry reinforcements were cautiously marching to Colber, no more than a few hours behind. The soldier's superior believed the supplies needed to reach Colber by that evening.

"I am surprised," the soldier concluded. "Gombder does not usually have many dangers during the day."

"Any other time, you would be correct," Uncle Timothy agreed and turned his gaze toward Lady Sheen. "Behemoth Toads are normally nocturnal. But it certainly appears we are the victims of changing times."

"Or just horrible fortune," Lady Sheen replied.

The caravan gathered their dead and wounded and tried to salvage all they could before heading onward to Colber. Lady Sheen held reservations about them moving on without the infantry, but she did not convey them. She believed they needed to meet up with the infantry and hasten them through Gombder.

17

The Woman of Beresdwell Wood

"I don't suppose you'd like to explain why that Behemoth Toads didn't turn us into breakfast?" Avaleigh asked as the Primitive Banes began finding their stride.

"I would like to know as well," Lady Sheen admitted.

Hayden gave his uncle a slight slap on his shoulder, urging him to explain. Uncle Timothy saw that he was nuzzled between the other two Primitive Banes—the one on the other side of him held curious yellow Goblin eyes.

"It would seem I am quite the oddity this morning," Uncle Timothy grinned. "The answer is simple of course. I cast a spell to conceal us from the sight of the monster after Hayden tried with all his might to expel the Behemoth with sheer force. However, sometimes the best way to defeat something so blubbery, where Thunder Strike cannot reach the nerves through its mass, is to hide."

"What spell did you cast?" Avaleigh irked. "Come on, tell us."

Uncle Timothy moved his memory back to his younger years, relaying his thoughts as he went. He didn't simply speak of the spell he learned, but of the Kingdom in which he learned it. His travels with his brother—Avaleigh and Hayden's father—took them to Walcook, a region made up of a variety of performance arts guilds, including ones that travel to the other three Kingdoms to seek fortune and renown. Walcook held rocky and green rolling foothills, with vast flowery meadows, and one large river running south to north. The region's main forest, the Beresdwell Wood, ran along it—the very place Uncle Timothy met a certain enchantress.

"Just a moment," Lady Sheen chimed in. "You're saying that you met the Enchantress of Beresdwell Wood?"

"She could have been a Witch of the Wilds," Uncle Timothy confessed. "But she was shrouded in light. Her hair sparkled in golden tresses with white and silver highlights. Her skin ran richly darkened, but shimmering like sunlight gleaming through stained glass. She was wrapped in white linen with a jeweled ruby necklace weighing heavily around her neck. And when she spoke to me, it resounded like harps echoing from afar."

Uncle Timothy and his brother decided to separate and explore Shaul, one of Walcook's major cities upon their arrival. The Festival of Lights, which depicts the end of winter and the beginning of spring, was a traditional festival just beginning when they arrived. It was an "up roaring jubilation that can deafen the senses" as Uncle Timothy described it. He felt the need to get away from the shoulder-to-shoulder crowds and wandered out of the city—into the forest and moving toward the sounds of roaring water. There, by the river, Uncle Timothy met her.

"You are not from Walcook," she said. "Yet I feel you know these woods."

"I do tend to feel at home among the trees," Uncle Timothy professed. His uneasiness did not go unnoticed. "It's peaceful—that is unless danger arises."

"Do you believe I'm dangerous?" The woman teased.

"You haven't brandished claws, unsheathed a blade, or tried to curse me yet," he teased in reply. "However, I do not usually run into women who appear the way you do."

"Your assumptions are fair," her demeanor became more stoic. "But I shall also say I have not felt one such as you enter here for many years. Thus, I have come to converse, if it shall not perturb you."

"We shall see," Uncle Timothy grinned.

His answers were brief at first to the woman's questions, such as where he hailed from, what his childhood was like, and how he began learning to cast. Yet as time passed, he became smitten and grew in desire to hear her voice, to know her thoughts, and to understand why she held such an interest in him. She did not hold back any of her curiosity.

They spoke through mid-day, only disturbed by the twittering of birds and squirrels at play. Then a stillness crept over the forest. The woman held up her hand to cease Uncle Timothy from speaking. Her head slowly turned, her eyes seeking the presence of a monster she had not revealed to her guest inhabited the wood. Uncle Timothy was not fooled by her light-hearted grin as she turned back toward his gaze.

"What is out there?" He whispered. He could see the woman's pause as she sifted past her reluctance.

"I don't know if I should tell you," she confessed. "I think it best to escort you out of the woods, back to where you shall remain safe."

"What is the alternative?" Uncle Timothy insisted.

"The monster that hunts nearby is rare and most deadly," she explained. "It is not likely you shall return if you seek it out, as many have tried, and all have failed."

"What is the reason for seeking it out?" Uncle Timothy asked.

"Power…power I have promised to the victor," the woman continued. "Powerful spells I have promised to casters for over one hundred years. One in the know of Nature, the other in Dusk."

"Would you teach me these spells if I defeat the monster?"

"You would receive all the knowledge of these spells in a single moment," the woman replied. "That is my power."

The price of risking his life and ridding the forest of the beast seemed reasonable to him. At the time, Uncle Timothy held a brash and bold approach to challenges, taking on high stakes to gain what he wanted most during that time in his life—knowledge and fame. He began stepping lightly away from the woman and turned back to flash her a cocky grin.

"I shall return," he promised. "Be sure you don't run off."

Uncle Timothy silently crept through the thicket, the shadows of the trees looming as one. The forest grew darker but rays of light continued to stab through the canopy just enough for him to peer ahead into the gloom. Though he remained vigilant and hidden, the glowing eyes of a monster of legend raised from the ground to peer in his direction. Uncle Timothy silenced his breathing following the resound of a low, chest-deep roar. He believed he had not been noticed and crept up the bulky tree he had been hiding behind just to be sure. A Manticore was on the hunt.

"I know not of anyone else who has seen one," Uncle Timothy confessed to Avaleigh and Hayden, with Lady Sheen and the Goblins gripped tightly to his story. "But someone had to have seen them before. Otherwise, how did I read about them in the books I read as a child? Sure enough, the beast sought out my flesh. Though by chance, I was downwind."

Of all conceivable accounts, Manticores—roughly translated as 'man-eaters'—show that the monsters do not go near inhabited areas, but instead remain hidden in high mountain peaks or dense forests, and it is believed that they are highly magical creatures with the intelligence to cast much like humans, speaking their own tongue to manifest their power. Their appearance contains the body of a lion, bat-like wings, and a long scorpion's tail. Uncle Timothy described it as such, with fur black like smoke and eyes that shimmered with a hue of blood-thirsty red.

MANTICORE

His ambush came sudden and precise, commanding a Thunder Strike that shot several lightning bolts through the canopy. The shadows of the forest were ripped from their hiding place, and so suddenly, the instant light of the sun blinded the monster for a moment. It felt the anguishing sting of electrical currents subduing it into paralysis. It thudded to the damp soil, writhing until it finally lay still. Uncle Timothy stood up just enough to peer at his results.

"I should have struck it again," he confessed. "Until it was ash."

The Manticore twitched back into consciousness with a roar that shook Uncle Timothy out of the tree. He landed with a hard thud and coughed loudly as if something had kicked him in the chest. The tree he was in had split in two, and he could see the Manticore slowly pacing its way toward him through the opening.

He did not wait to conjure another spell, knowing it had become too late to flee. Uncle Timothy brought forth a Stormy Gale that slowed the monster for a moment while he sped off to find another spot to hide, believing he needed another opportunity to ambush the beast. However, he could hear the Manticore's roar closing in behind him and in the thicket of the forest, Uncle Timothy knew he would not last for long. He made his way to the river and leaped into the rushing water just in time before the large paws of the beast could tear him asunder. He turned to see the beast giving him chase along the shoreline. It leaped into the air and began to soar above him.

Uncle Timothy was not pleased with his predicament. He plunged underwater as the monster drew closer. He cast Stormy Gale that burst out of the water and slammed into the beast hovering above his position. The Manticore made an enormous splash into the river and swept on by. Uncle Timothy pushed his head above the water gasping for air and saw the Manticore trying to swim against the current that picked up a peculiar speed, meaning only one thing— they were approaching a waterfall.

No branches or rocks could cease him from going over. Uncle Timothy watched the Manticore go over first, but the beast spread out its wings and soared into the air.

"Blast!" Uncle Timothy said aloud to himself. "Straight into the jaws."

He felt his body suddenly begin to fall, and just as it did, the Manticore struck, biting down on his face, and lifting him into the sky. What the monster did not know came as the spell Uncle Timothy cast just before going over the falls.

"It's the only Gravity spell I know," he explained to his niece and nephew. "I will teach it to you in time but—Fortify saved my life."

The spell places an invisible barrier around the caster, protecting them from physical harm for a time. The more mastery of the spell, the greater strength the barrier becomes. And Uncle Timothy thanked his father for teaching it to him as a boy, practicing it each day to grow the spell to be mightily manifested within himself, strong enough to stop a Manticore's bite.

But Uncle Timothy now had a new problem. His head was stuck in the monster's mouth with the spell draining his stamina. Should he tire, he would surely lose his head to the monster's jaws. Casting another spell would tire him further, and if the Manticore didn't release him, his life could end rather unpleasantly.

A stroke of fortune came when the beast took him upward, higher into the heavens, and opened its jaws to get a better grip. But Uncle Timothy slipped his head out, plummeting at an increasing speed toward the forest below. It had been a clever move on the Manitcore's part, knowing that the caster's spell would soon wear off, and he would have nowhere else to go but his doom.

"I didn't know I was going to get a flying lesson today," Uncle Timothy nervously chuckled as he tumbled through the air.

The Manticore plunged with him and began to reach out with its jaws again. Uncle Timothy did not waste time casting a Stormy Gale to gust the monster away from him. He refused to perish by its bite and accepted his fate from the fall. Yet to his surprise, a large Cyclone cradled him to the ground. His vision was spinning but even in his dizziness, he recognized the one who had rescued him. "Well met brother," Uncle Timothy huffed.

"I knew you would likely take a walk in these woods," his brother replied. "I did not know you would end up facing something like that."

"I'll explain later," Uncle Timothy said. "Right now, the Manticore comes."

What trouble a single caster might have faced alone against a Manticore became lessened by the presence of another. Richard, Uncle Timothy's youngest brother, was fresh and at ease. While Uncle Timothy caught his breath. Richard, though a man built thinner than Uncle Timothy's bulk, remained just as strong in his casting. His wild bluish eyes remained calm, practically welcoming the challenge of survival—with a slight grin neatly tucked beneath his golden beard. His high fade swerved into a textured mess of thick hair slightly curving upward. He ran his fingers through it with a conceited sigh and suddenly brought forth a larger Sinister Cyclone than before. The spell swirled and picked up water from the river, making its way in the path of the Manticore flying hastily toward them. With a roar, the beast dispelled the Cyclone and continued its path.

"That's just impolite," Richard scoffed. "Don't suppose you could join with me in a Gale, brother?"

The two brothers cast a Stormy Gale together, which made it seem like the Manticore slammed into a wall of chilling winds. As if it were yanked from the sky, it fell to the forest floor below, in a dense covering of trees from the sight of the brothers. They waited patiently. Dusk was settling, and the Manticore emerged into the clearing where the two stood. Uncle Timothy had enough time to catch his breath and began feeling a renewed strength, while Richard again took the lead. With their staffs in hand, they watched the Manticore roar, breaking the trees around it, and the brothers could feel the surge of its shockwave into the ground. They quickly regained their footing, ignoring the aching in their chests to greet the onslaught of the charging beast. The Manticore suddenly stopped in its tracks, now gazing upon several others who looked just like Richard. Uncle Timothy had moved behind them.

While his father taught his brother the Gravity Spell of Fortify, Richard's mother was teaching him the Conjuring Spell, Replica—allowing the caster to duplicate themselves and overpower or outnumber an opponent. Growth and mastery of the spell allowed the caster to generate more numbers of themselves with increases in agility. And Richard had been a prodigy in this regard. More than one hundred copies stood and surrounded the beast, but also concealed his brother who was summoning all the power he could muster within himself. The Manticore charged and bit clean through a duplicate, and in its demise became like chaff in the wind. Again, the Manticore struck, this time with its scorpion tail, sending yet another to become debris. The replicas began moving around it, taunting, and sacrificing themselves to its savagery. Yet it remained unable to taste human flesh.

Richard's replicas suddenly pounced on the monster, climbing aboard its back, and recklessly grasping its tail and wings. The Manticore became enticingly mad with rage that it did not notice the spark erupting from Uncle Timothy's hands. The replicas pushed away, many destroyed as they retreated, but the electrical current found its mark. Once more, the beast fell into paralysis. Uncle Timothy focused his Thunder Strike brilliantly as his brother, Richard, hoisted the Manticore upward in a Sinister Cyclone. While paralyzed, the monster flew high into the air and mercilessly fell to its doom upon the clearing floor. Its back burst open as it landed, spilling a dark crimson among the rocky shoreline of the river. Uncle Timothy approached it, aimed another Thunder Strike into its open eyes, and destroyed everything that remained inside its skull.

"The champion has a sibling," the brothers heard a woman's voice suddenly behind them.

"I care not for your prize, my lady," Uncle Timothy replied, which manifested bewilderment in the woman. "While my head was stuck within the creature's mouth, I realized I never should have taken on such a feat alone. I am fortunate to have such a brother."

"Then should I give your brother the prize?" She asked.

"You will give us both the prize," Richard interjected. "The hearsay of the locals tell of a woman who appears in the wood each year during the Festival of Lights. They say she entices men, whether casters or not, to fight this thing, promising them power and fame. But really, it is just to feed them to her beast. I knew my brother would not be able to resist walking these woods. Thus, I came looking for him."

"How you found him so quickly is impressive," the woman scowled. "We've practiced tracking one another down our whole lives," Richard chuckled. "Though, I was always the better at hide and seek."

"Whatever the reason is," the woman huffed. "I have made my vow to whoever fell the beast shall receive two spells, one in the knowledge of nature, the other in Dusk. Yet since there are two champions, and the prize cannot be split, I shall allow each one of you to decide the gifts I bestow upon the other. It is only fair as you exploited such a loophole."

"I know the spells you need, brother," Richard laughed.

"Twisting Twilight is the Dusk spell my brother chose for me, one that would allow me to be better at hide and seek," Uncle Timothy chuckled, seeing his niece and nephew enthralled with the ending to his tale.

"Twisting Twilight?" Avaleigh interjected. "Is that the spell you used?"

"Yes," Uncle Timothy replied. "The spell bends the appearance of one's surroundings, having the capability of making others see what the caster wishes. It's focused on bending light without the use of mirrors or other parlor tricks."

"What was the Nature spell?" Lady Sheen jumped in.

"Commune," Uncle Timothy replied.

18
Malevolence From the Dark

"I was unaware your family held such power," Lady Sheen said. "Nor did I conceive you were a Witch of the Wilds."

"Long ago," Uncle Timothy corrected. "Your father knows but never speaks of it—the same as the Queen's father knew before him. Many of us who wanted peace became casters and conducted our business in the services of Essend's King."

"Do you hide such a thing out of fear?" Avaleigh asked.

"To keep others from being afraid, yes," Uncle Timothy concurred. "When people learn of such a thing, they are often reluctant to offer any sort of hospitality. And men raised in that fear test their brawn as their prejudice blinds them."

"Tell us more about the Nature spell you learned." Lady Sheen jumped in. "And what of your brother? What spells did you choose for him?"

Commune is a Nature spell that allows the caster to commune with animals. Since no spell is alike, in this way, a caster may find it easier to be friendlier with some species than others. A caster can also grow in knowledge to befriend what some refer to as monsters. Uncle Timothy explained it was not apparent to him from the beginning what animals or monsters he would commune best with—he promised to relay that tale another time.

"I chose Timber Harvest as the Nature spell for my brother," Uncle Timothy said. "While I find trees peaceful and pleasant, my brother assuredly has always seen them as alive, whispering as if the winds carried their thoughts to his ears. The spell I chose for him gave my brother power over root systems and how they function. Likely, as the caster progresses in mastery of the Timber Harvest spell, much larger roots can be controlled in such a way it would seem like the trees come to life."

"You are truly insightful," Lady Sheen chuckled. "What was the Dusk spell you chose for him?"

"Shadow Pull," Uncle Timothy replied, his face becoming more stoic, and his eyes turned further to the road ahead. "As my brother chose something for me to be better at hide and seek, I decided I would return the favor. Shadow Pull allows the caster to bend the appearance of shadows, while also manipulating them into a 'portal' like system, giving the caster the ability to jump through one shadow and out another."

Their conversing became interrupted by Dundlen's infantry approaching them, marching at an even pace. Uncle Timothy had spotted them first and shifted Lady Sheen's and the others' attention in their direction. The approach of the Primitive Bane Riders was welcomed most honorably by two commanders, each one in charge of a brigade of at least one thousand strong. They stopped to greet one another along the road, in the clearing between the forests of Gombder and Ogrin, surrounded by shimmering wetlands blossoming meadow grass, and a natural spring that only reveals itself after the winter thaws.

Essend holds no major rivers to speak of, as many of its rivers run underground, but the land provides hundreds of places to retrieve fresh water—many of which can be found near Ogrin and Gombder, also along the roads between Holprice and Shroe. Remel's Bay is practically all fresh water and provides some of the best farmland in the kingdom.

But it was not the land where Avaleigh and Hayden placed their gaze—it was the soldiers of Dundlen. All were dressed in grey-plated armor, with chainmail lying beneath. Like the Primitive Riders, Dundlen's soldiers were distinctly set apart from others in the King's service—an elite trained infantry. The majority of soldiers clung to broad shields, their spears sharpened to excellence, and likely the same could be said of their swords sheathed at their sides. Others held halberds or bows, but each one wore a bright sapphire paludamentum (the same as Lady Sheen) with the emblem of the golden stag. Lady Sheen brought her Primitive Bane forward, and the two commanders who had stepped out to greet them removed their helms. Their aura was that of brothers, strength in their stance and a united bow to Lady Sheen.

The first commander had short dirty blonde hair, tightened to the sides, and a neat uneven surface upon his dome soaked in sweat from the wearing of his helm. His eyes were almond-shaped, with skin that held to a tawny hue. His build held that of noble stature though he stood no taller than a normal man. Yet he appeared formidable among all the troops who stood in line. His hands rested on his uniquely engraved hilt—undoubtedly a family heirloom.

The second commander stood only slightly shorter, but his shoulders carried the broadness of a bred warrior, and his eyes held a piercing gaze of one who had seen many battles. He shook the sweat from his short brown hair, his skin lighter than his other, but revealed it was capable of slowly bronzing in the light of the sun. The sword at his side held more of a curved sheathe than his fellow commander, a weapon likely for tighter quarters, which revealed he preferred to be in the midst of the fray.

"Most honorable greetings to you, Lady Sheen," the first commander said. "If I could inquire, why are you traveling away from Colber?"

"We were in desperate need to know if our messengers had reached Dundlen," Lady Sheen replied. "We were traveling through Gombder and helped the ones you sent ahead of you. Your caravan of supplies ran into a large problem as they were making haste."

"Behemoth Toads!" Hayden interjected.

"That is troubling news," the second commander stated, ignoring the boy's insolence, as he noticed Lady Sheen had done the same.

"Were there any casualties?"

"Quite a few," Lady Sheen replied. "But we were able to fend off the monsters. However, they may still be lurking along the road. I suggest making camp before trekking through Gombder. Colber is well-defended, and shall welcome the relief once you arrive."

"Thank you, my Lady," the first commander replied. "I am Commander Michael. This is Commander David. Should you wish to make camp with us tonight, you would be most welcome."

"We welcome the company as well," Uncle Timothy tilted his head downward in respect. "Where would you like us?"

"We'll create an encircled encampment," Commander Michael motioned. "Like always, the broad shields creating an outer rim of defense and archers on alert just behind them. Please make your encampment and rest more toward the center."

It took some time for Lady Sheen to explain Hayden's condition, but the soldiers of Dundlen remained unshaken when dusk came, and Jasper became visibly floating just behind the boy. Despite the curse, the soldiers appeared more at ease seeing Lady Sheen traveling with casters. They did, however, sneer at the Goblins in their company. Though Grug and his two kin were not at fault, Dundlen and the Goblin tribes of the West were not adhering to peaceful terms. No word of war was ever spoken, but the tribe to the north, in the mountains above Ogrin were no strangers to stealing from Dundlen soldiers patrolling the coast beyond Byre. And the Goblin tribe to the southwest, which lived on the coast, often looted ships under cover of darkness in Arwal. But they mostly whispered of the Gnoll tribes uniting.

The sun scarcely shined through the tree trunks of Ogrin when a loud alert disturbed the silence of the twilight. Both commanders urged Lady Sheen and the others to remain where they were. Yet Lady Sheen followed Michael to the south where his troops were stationed in defense. David traveled to the north with Uncle Timothy in tow, who had strictly told the two young casters to remain with the Grug.

"What are those shadows in the distance?" Hayden pointed toward the north.

"They appear to be the same as the ones to the south," Avaleigh replied.

"Those numbers are vast," Grug interjected. "But they're not tall enough to be Gnolls."

Grug soon corrected himself as more numbers followed in behind the shorter silhouettes, undoubtedly the beasts that sieged Colber days before. Their numbers swarmed all around them with the smaller shadows marching in front. Grug climbed atop his Primitive Bane and could scarcely catch his breath from the shock that caught his eyes. The smaller shadows were Goblins, painted for war—the tribes of the west.

The enemy's lines halted just beyond the reach of Dundlen's bows. The sea of Goblins and Gnolls parted in several places as Grug was joined by Avaleigh and Hayden upon the Primitive Bane. To their astonishment, lines of Gnolls came trotting down, mounted on their steed of choice—Ripmaws. Such monsters are known to be

throughout the four kingdoms and are bear-like in size, power, and held violent tempers. Their massive jaws could 'unlock' and extend to take on larger animals. While Ripmaws in the wild primarily are hunters for prey such as fish and other animals, Ripmaws under the training of Gnolls appeared to have a more select palette, one for human flesh. Their black-bluish, prickly fur now practically hid them in the growing darkness.

Lady Sheen and Uncle Timothy were suddenly hurrying to mount their Primitive Banes. The two commanders could be heard shouting orders in the distance, and hundreds of torches were suddenly lit as the light of the land struggled to remain.

"There's no moon tonight," Uncle Timothy said. "We shall be in total darkness."

"We don't have to be," Hayden retorted. "You and I can cast Thunder Strikes to help scatter them. I can focus on the south and you can focus on the north."

"Spoken like a true lead caster," Uncle Timothy smiled.

"I can create a moat around us," Avaleigh chimed in.

"This shall be your greatest test of strength yet," Uncle Timothy sighed. "Don't stop casting until I tell you."

"What shall we do?" Grug asked.
"Stay close to me," Lady Sheen answered. "And put these on so that you are not mistaken for the enemy."

She handed the Goblins three charcoal-colored cloaks with Essend's emblem of the golden stag, to which they quickly slipped them on. Morlo and Porlo climbed aboard their Primitive Bane with their bows in hand, and Grug took up the reins. Lady Sheen clasped a newly acquired spear, courtesy of Dundlen's Commander Michael, and also clutched a buckler in her left hand. Her other weapons, a rapier and short sword remained sheathed in the saddle of her Primitive Bane.

"We stay in the center," she explained, her eyes shooting toward Uncle Timothy. "All of us. Should there come a time where we can break through and escape toward Dundlen, I command that we take it."

Uncle Timothy made no argument, but prepared his sights, setting toward the north. Hayden felt Avaleigh swiftly wrap her arms around him before easing her grip.

"Don't die on this one," her voice trembled with concern. "You are strong enough. You don't need to overdo it."

"There's a Tremor of Power to the west," Hayden grinned. "If you kill more than me, you can have it."

The boy's Thunder Strike was already powering up, and he cast it into the skies overhead to the south, lighting up the night just in time for Commander Michael's soldiers to see the coming onslaught of Goblins and Gnolls. The monsters charged into the three-stacked high shield wall of Dundlen's elite, and even with such strength slamming into them like a riptide, the infantry's line did not budge. Arrows flew over their heads and rained down upon the monsters sacrificing their lives and limbs trying to break through the Dundlen soldiers defenses.

To the north, the skies lit up with lightning as Uncle Timothy cast his Thunder Strike. Commander David's troops braced for much of the same as their comrades facing the south. And then to the west, the east—suddenly, Dundlen's infantry began to struggle on all sides, holding the circle, and mercilessly thrusting spears outward into Gnoll and Goblin alike.

The fray dispersed, with the Gnolls and Goblins fleeing, not out of fear, but to deploy the new foe. They had tested the might of Dundlen's shields, and the brawn of its infantry's tenacity. Now the Ripmaws stepped forward as the skies grew dark again.

"Cast another Thunder Strike," Uncle Timothy motioned to Hayden.

"This time let the bolts fall."

"What if I misjudge the distance?" Hayden replied. "Before there were only monsters in a courtyard, now there are allies in front of me."

"Aim for the back of the horde," Avaleigh encouraged him. "You'll likely hit something and slow them."

"What about you?" Hayden scoffed. "Didn't you say you were going to cast a moat around us all?"

"I will," Avaleigh teased. "I'm waiting until the precise moment."

Hayden ignored her and lit up the skies again to the south. But she received an empowering nod from her uncle, seeing she was already gathering vapor to her. The air began to loom with mist, rolling in where Dundlen's infantry took its stand. Before the Ripmaws could charge, a fog formed, but only reached ankle high. When the monsters charged carrying their growling Gnoll warriors, the beasts suddenly splashed deep into loose soil and churned it to muck. Gnolls that landed near the lines of the Dundlen were rapidly pierced with several spears.

An unexpected Stormy Gale began to blow. The icy winds hardened the murky waters Avaleigh had created, and the horde charged again. Uncle Timothy turned his eyes southward, spotting a figure in the shadows, too far to make out who or what it was—but for certain, it held a glowing staff that seemed familiar. The figure crept back into the night, and Uncle Timothy knew his attention was needed elsewhere. The second charge of the horde came on stronger than before, and the lines of Dundlen suddenly began to break.

Gnolls and Goblins burst through the lines, mercilessly slaughtering archers trying to defend themselves. The shield walls could no longer hold, and they began to falter. Fortunately, Hayden had yet to let his bolts of lightning descend from the sky. He did so as the soldiers scrambled to retreat and regroup. And the power of his Thunder Strike erupted into the lines of Gnolls and Goblins, slowing them enough to allow Commander Michael to order the reforming of the shield walls. Uncle Timothy followed the example of his nephew, dropping his bolts of lightning as the shield wall broke in the north. Commander David retreated his soldiers and regrouped into another shield wall. The circle of Dundlen had shrunk, leaving their dead to remain where they fell, and left no choice for their wounded to join them. The Gnolls and Goblins ripped, bashed, and clawed at any Dundlen soldier that remotely twitched.

"This is not how it shall end!" Hayden screamed. His cast of Sinister Cyclone brought forth hesitation from the monsters looking to continue their attack.

Uncle Timothy's gaze caught something toward the east, the same shadowy figure lit up by the light of his casting, though closer now, its staff glowing once more. Hayden's Sinister Cyclone began to pick up momentum when another whirlwind, much swifter than his, collided with his cyclone and dispersed it.

Avaleigh saw the shadowy figure as well. For once, she was thankful for Hayden's hotblooded retaliation. After witnessing his cyclone outmatched, he cast Thunder Strike again to light up the skies, enabling her to make out more details of the elongated human figure, manifesting mists of smoke and darkness around its body. She could see its armor, black with a smooth, faceless helm, jagged gauntlets, a severely torn cloak, and intricate glyphs intertwined throughout the body of the plate covering. The dark figure carried a flail hanging from a chain and a caster's staff with the head of a drake. The body of the staff appeared as an elongation and twisting of the drake's torso, ending in a sharpened point at the staff's tail.

Hayden's eyes pulsed and a rush of power shook his body. Jasper took to the skies above the boy and in an instant Hayden became transported above the battlefield, suspended in midair like a bird hovering on the air currents, and specter wings weaved their way from his backside. Lightning struck his staff, and he propelled it downward, with each strand ripping through the enemy's lines. The Goblins appeared to take the brunt of the boy's electric bombardment, and each monster stumbled into a full retreat.

The shadow figure had faded from sight, leaving only Avaleigh with her imagination of who the figure could have been. Uncle Timothy sighed heavily when she told him of what she saw, and to his knowledge, it sounded like a powerful specter, much like the Bonecrackle mage.

"It was not a specter," Jasper's voice interjected. Uncle Timothy and Avaleigh peered up from their conversation as Hayden moved toward them, appearing weary and ready to pass out.

"Dundlen is not far," Lady Sheen said. "But this is where I leave you. I must travel back with the reinforcements and ensure Colber remains strong."

"You have been generous in your help, my lady," Uncle Timothy replied. "I shall ensure another message is sent to you once we reach Dundlen."

The push through Ogrin Forest held little resistance, with only one Primitive Bane growing ill from fatigue. Yet they rested the beast well and soon they were able to hastily pass beyond the treeline and saw Dundlen on the horizon. Uncle Timothy's eyes grew wide when they gazed upon the city as did Grug and the rest of the goblins.

"What is it?" Hayden asked.

"Smoke rises heavily from Dundlen," he answered. "They were attacked recently, likely a day or so before we arrived."

They pressed onward, cautiously approaching the city, and found relief seeing Dundlen soldiers still occupying and fortifying its defenses.

"You know, we never did go get you that Tremor of Power," Hayden told Avaleigh.

"Didn't you kill more than me? I believe it goes to you," she replied.

"But we pick it up on our way home."

"Not sure when that shall be," Hayden admitted. "We may be doing this for a while. However, I wish to still make sure you get the next one."

Avaleigh smiled at her brother, who sounded more like one of the commanders they met from Dundlen. Yet one thing they both knew—they were far from home.

Monster Glossary

Ash Hounds

Found throughout the four Kingdoms, Ash Hounds are the only canines known to breathe fire. They have dark gray fur with streaks of violet and are extremely aggressive, but travel in packs of no more than six. While they may appear frail due to their unusually thin appearance, their strength is not to be underestimated as they only harbor an estimated one percent of body fat, and their skin is almost as dense as bone.

Behemoth Toads

Found throughout the four Kingdoms, Behemoth Toads are massive amphibians that remain close to swamplands or murky waters. Goblins are their main course, as Goblins stick close to these domains as well. However, these creatures don't hesitate to shoot their tongue out to nab whatever they deem to be food. While it is not known how many are left in the wilds, as Goblins have done their best to kill them off, they continue to keep Goblin numbers in check.

Blighttalons (blite · ta · luhns):

Found throughout the four Kingdoms, Blighttalons are birds of prey, most closely related to eagles, but on a much larger scale. They are rare and carry the ability to cast "Sinister Cyclone" with the flap of their wings. They are mostly white with black streaks running through their feathers, with black talons and beaks, and are immune to electrical currents. Their wingspan is approximately sixteen to eighteen feet, and luckily do not appear to see humans as much of a meal.

Bonecrackle (bohn · kra · kl) Caster

Much like Bonecrackles that are abominations of bones not properly laid to rest, a Bonecrackle Caster is an improperly laid to rest caster who either died violently, foolishly by their own hand, or a curse of some kind. It is rare a Bonecrackle Caster comes about, but are formidable whenever faced.

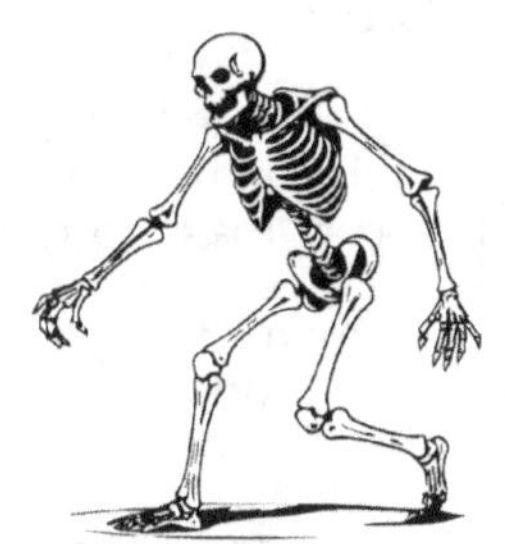

Bonecrackles (bohn · kra · kls)

Found throughout the four Kingdoms, Bonecrackles are abominations of bones not properly laid to rest. Surprisingly, not found in graveyards. Bonecrackles are bare skeletons that rise from the earth only at night. Legends depict them as forgotten spells manifested by Witches of the Wilds to prevent people from venturing into their domain.

Brutal Swine

Found throughout the four Kingdoms, Brutal Swines are wild boars (pigs) that can grow into the size of a Savage Howler. They are made up of a variety of hues like black and dark brown, but more commonly are more of a lighter brown. Some may even be spotted with black with their light brown hides. Their tusks and horns do not cease growing throughout their lifetime, and their hooves are razor sharp. While extremely aggressive, they are unintelligent, and are not above charging at anything. Often the steeds of Goblin tribes.

Glowserpents (glo · ser · pent)

Found throughout the four Kingdoms, Glowserpents are large, carnivorous snakes that have the ability to cast "Thunder Strike" spells, glowing bright gold through their skin just before they are about to strike. While not all Glowserpents' Thunder Strikes are deadly, they do paralyze what is stricken, just for enough time to be wrapped in the serpent's coils. Goblins refer to them as "The Naga Necroman."

Gnolls (nol · es)

Found throughout the four Kingdoms, Gnolls are a war-minded race of vicious but simple-minded hyena-like humanoids. Though highly aggressive, Gnolls are notorious for being extremely unintelligent and prone to infighting, and love to let others do the hard work for them. Most tribes are mainly found in Autumnwich and do not have a love for caves or those who dwell within them.

Goblins (more specifically Grug)

Found throughout the four Kingdoms, Goblins are tribe-minded humanoid creatures that inhabit mostly marshes and swamps. They breed in mass to grow their numbers to war against Gnoll tribes, Spitwasps, and even humans. They range in a variety of hues, green to black, and are mercilessly aggressive in battle, regardless of their gender. Much like the people of Autumnwich, the average height of Goblins is of shorter stature, reaching no more than 4.5 feet.

Manticore (man · ti · cor)

Found throughout the four Kingdoms, Manticores are rare creatures with the body of a lion, bat-like wings, and a long scorpion's tail. Roughly translated, Manticore means "man-eater." Most accounts show Manticores do not go near inhabited areas, but instead remain hidden in high mountain peaks or dense forests. It is believed that they are highly magical creatures with the intelligence to cast much like human casters, speaking their own tongue to manifest their power.

Primitive Bane (prim · it · iv | bain)

Found only in Essend, Primitive Banes bulky primate creatures standing at least twice the height of any normal man, with black fur, sharp fangs, a grip that can easily crush bones or rip apart most things, even iron bars. Wild Primitive Banes mainly inhabit Essend's largest forests, Ogrin and Gombder. Colber is known for domesticating them as steeds, using them for hauling trade goods within the "Trade Triangle" that includes Colber, Arwal, and Prave.

Ripmaw

Found throughout the four kingdoms, Ripmaws are bear-like creatures with prickly fur and violent tempers. Their massive claws are retractable on all four of their paws, and their jaws can unlock to extend further down. While most of their prey are fish and other animals, Ripmaws are known to attack humans without reason. Their fur ranges from black to bluish hues, but some are majestically gold, and is the choice of steed for Gnolls.

Savage Howler (sa • vuhj | hau • lr)

Found throughout the four Kingdoms, these monsters are large, lone canines, until it's mating season. Their fur is grayish in tone but often has golden streaks running up and down like pinstripes. Savage Howlers give off a loud howl once they've made a kill almost as if they're boasting about what they've done.

Scaley Dread (skay • lee | dred)

Found near rivers and lakes in Essend, Flemder, and Walcook, Scaley Dreads are semi-aquatic reptiles appearing much like alligators or crocodiles. They range in all different sizes with the largest one ever recorded as fifty-two feet long, snout to tail. They are spotted creatures, made up of grays and blacks, with pointy scales armoring the top of their head and body.

Spitwasp (spit • waasp)

Found throughout the four Kingdoms, Spitwasps are large wasp-like creatures (about the size of a Goblin). They are striped gold and black down their torso and build giant mud nests in swamps. While colonies of Spitwasps vary, it is rare to see a nest of more than fifty to sixty at a time. Their food source is the meat of pretty much any kind, and they are mostly scavengers unless they see Goblins walking about.

Warptooths (warp • tooths)

Found throughout the four Kingdoms, Warptooths are four-legged canine creatures with protruding, jagged teeth. Their fur is sleek and usually gray or mildly dark brown. A Warptooth has a great deal of speed but lacks the stamina to run long distances. They can be clever and are respectful hunters. Some are domesticated as pets, but most of them remain in packs in the wilds.

SHOW YOUR SUPPORT FOR
SELF-PUBLISHING AUTHORS

Enjoying The Goolwind Tales? Support this and more self-published works from this author by visiting Amazon.com, PublishersBrew.com and click "leave a book review," or your favorite digital book platform where this volume is sold.

ACKNOWLEDGMENTS

A special thanks first and foremost to my Abba in heaven for giving me the creative mind and the inspiration to share this work. He is the light of my life and my greatest treasure. I acknowledge his sovereignty and His goodness, and give Him many thanks for my family, both through blood and through spirit.

To my two beautiful children, Avaleigh & Hayden—may this story be enjoyed by you all the days of your life, and may you know how much I love you with every word you read of this series. It is my gift to you.

My heart goes out to the love of my life, my beautiful bride, Jennifer. Thank you for your support and keeping my confidence grounded. I thank Abba for you every day that you were created, and that you continue to cheer me on. Forever and always, I love you.

Finally, I would like to thank you reader, for supporting me and self-published authors like me who desire to craft stories from the heart of their imagination, and not for corporations just to turn a profit. Your support is worth more than you'll ever know, and it gives writers and artists like me the ability to pursue our passions in world building.

ABOUT THE AUTHOR

Born and raised in Chico, California, Ricky Hayes holds degrees in Journalism and Graphic Design, and has worked on the creative side of Web Development and Marketing for well over a decade. He is an award-winning poet and has branched out into self-publishing for numerous years, even before Amazon bought Create Space. He is the owner of Publisher's Brew, an aspiring author alliance established in 2022 for self-publishing authors but also maintains his passion for designing beautiful websites for clients.

In January of 2009, Ricky's mom passed away from ALS, which he believes marked his life to begin pursuing writing more passionately, as she remained his greatest encouragement until leaving this world behind.

Some of Ricky's favorite authors are Jules Verne, R. A. Salvatore, J.R.R. Tolkien, C.S. Lewis, Kenneth Grahame, and Paul Zindel.